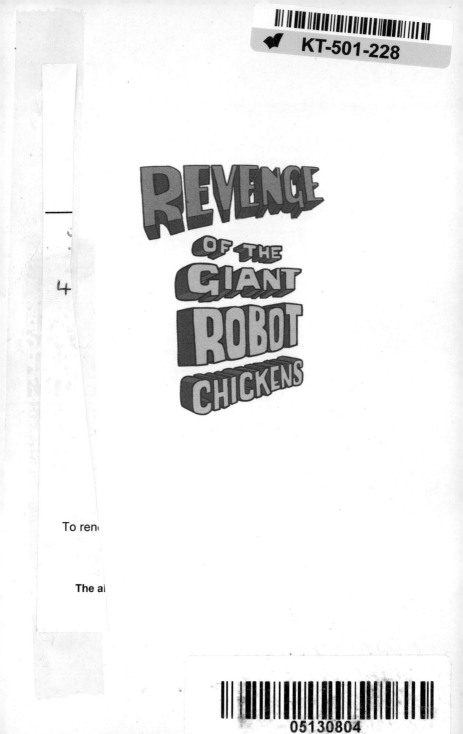

REVENGE
OF THE
GIANT
ROBOT
CHICKENS

To ren

The a

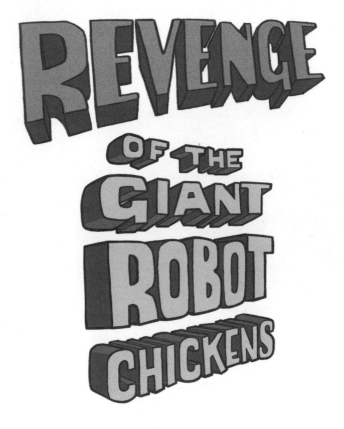

REVENGE OF THE GIANT ROBOT CHICKENS

ALEX McCALL

 Kelpies

Kelpies is an imprint of Floris Books
First published in 2015 by Floris Books

The publisher acknowledges subsidy from
Creative Scotland towards the publication
of this volume

 This book is also available
as an eBook

British Library CIP data available
ISBN 978-178250-210-4
Printed in Poland

This book is dedicated to Mum, Dad and Lucy, who put up with me. Despite everything.

CHAPTER 1

I stared in dismay as Sam was plucked into the air. Our eyes met and I could see the desperation in them, the fear. Then, with a flick of the neck that I'd become too familiar with, he was tossed backwards and swallowed whole.

"Scatter," I yelled at the rest of my squad, but they were way ahead of me. From the moment the enormous chicken had burst through their trap they'd gone running in every direction. I stared after them for a moment. I had hoped that at least one would have stood and fought.

Then the chicken turned its attention to me and I sprinted after them as fast as I could.

The ground began to shake as the chicken chased me, its metal wings spread, and it let out the shrill screech that haunted my dreams each night. If I got to the backup position in time I might make it. If not, I'd soon be joining Sam.

I jinked down a narrow side street, the houses beginning to close in about me. The chicken could still fit in, I knew it could, but it would be a squeeze. That would slow it down and give me a better chance.

The chicken entered the street when I was halfway up. Perhaps it was a novice; it didn't manage the turn properly and crashed into one of the buildings. Bricks showered down around me and a blossom of dust raced up the street. I held my breath for a moment and glanced up. Any moment now.

There was a shout, and heads appeared in upper windows. The nets we'd developed over the last few months glistened in the air as they were tossed over the beast. If our plan worked as I'd hoped, the nets should stop it. But I kept running anyway.

It was a good thing I did. Even inexperienced, this chicken was deadly. Its head snapped round, eyes glowing red. It dodged the first net and zapped the second with its laser eyes. With the beams still engaged, it swung its head round, cutting through the first-floor rooms around it. I wasn't too worried; everyone had orders to get out of the way as soon as the nets had been flung. And, as the rapid thumping from behind reminded me, I was still being pursued.

I hadn't done a lot of running before the chicken apocalypse. I hadn't really needed to. But when your world has been taken over by giant robot chickens you sort of lose the choice. My new trainers held the ground, pushing me forward. I needed to gain as much distance as I could while the chicken was distracted.

At the end of the street was a little roundabout.

I turned left, as I'd practised over the last few days, into another street, wider than the last.

We'd learned a lot in the past two months. Ever since the Battle of Pittodrie – when we outwitted the chickens, taking down their signal mast in Aberdeen – we'd had a little more freedom to plan our defence.

I managed to get through the street and into a small square before the chicken reached the roundabout. Pausing before a long-dead car I stopped and looked back, allowing myself a smile.

The chicken came into the road at a dead run. It was going so fast, it wasn't able to stop when it saw the trip wires we'd spread across the street. Long ago I'd tried to use one made of rope, wrapped around lampposts. The image of the chicken ripping its way through them was another thing I kept seeing in my dreams. That's why these were steel cables, attached to the walls.

I thought I glimpsed the moment the chicken realised it had been tricked. I grinned at it, mockingly. It would fall and then we'd trap and disable it.

My grin lasted until it bent its knees and jumped, fire blasting out from under its tail feathers sending it soaring over the street. It landed behind me and I turned in shock. It cocked its head to the side and glared beadily at me.

The others think I'm crazy when I say I can see expressions in the robots' faces. They say it's impossible for a solid metal mask to show emotion. But they're wrong. You can totally tell what a chicken is feeling, and this one was smug. It knew it had won and it was gloating.

Until it heard a faint whining sound.

Kids swarmed out of the side streets, hefting heavy guns: long tubes with the image of a chicken's face mounted on the front. The eyes glowed, bright cherry red. One of them fired into the ground just by the chicken's feet, the laser leaving a smoking hole in the ground.

Yeah, we'd learned a lot in the past few months.

A diminutive figure clambered onto the roof of one of the cars. He stood there, legs spread wide, long coat flapping in the wind. I felt my eyes narrow. Cody.

"Fly away birdie," he taunted.

The robot looked at him, then around at the kids with their lasers glowing. It spread its wings and began to flap, hopping up and down. I knew that movement.

"No!" I yelled, running forward. But I was too late. In a moment the chicken lifted off the ground. It turned once in the air then headed north, over the rooftops and away from the city.

Everyone around the square relaxed and turned off their lasers. I stormed over to Cody just as he was jumping down from his car-top perch.

"Why did you let it get away?" I yelled at him. "It had Sam."

He looked at me with expressionless eyes. They had made me shiver the first time I met him and they made me shiver now. I had just learned not to show it.

"If we'd taken it down we'd have risked hurting him. We couldn't do it safely. We had no choice."

"You could have shot off its legs. You could have done *something*!"

But even as I said it I knew he was right. The chickens didn't harm their human captives, just kept them imprisoned, so Sam should be fine. Cody seemed to recognise this because he didn't say anything, just changed the subject.

"Any word lately?"

All my anger suddenly drained away – my rage at Cody, at the chickens, at everything, suddenly deflating – as I remembered my best friend. "No, not for a day or two," I said. "But he'll probably contact me sooner or later."

"Four days, by my count," Cody replied, and suddenly I couldn't meet his eyes. I turned and stared at the kids packing up, laughing together at surviving yet another day. I felt his hand on my shoulder.

"I'm sorry, Rayna," Cody said.

I turned, shocked. It was so out of character for him to be sympathetic. I almost thought I'd imagined it. But he was gone, walking back to his team, getting ready to move them to the next stronghold.

I picked up my pack from the car I'd left it in and settled it firmly on my shoulders. Taking a deep breath, I turned south and started walking towards the train station. It would be my job to give his gang the news about Sam.

Man, I really missed Jesse.

CHAPTER 2

JESSE: Operation Henhouse Hustle

Why did the chicken go camping?

He didn't. Camping is rubbish.

Every so often Dad used to make some attempt to get me to appreciate the great outdoors. This involved random trips to distant corners of Scotland, cut off from a comfy bed, all my favourite television shows and the internet. Without fail we'd be woken at the crack of dawn by birds that seemed to take the idea of us having a good night's sleep as a personal insult. Dad would get up, stick his head out of the tent and inhale deeply. He'd usually follow this up with commenting on how you didn't get air like this back at home. If we'd lived in a city, that would make sense, but we didn't. We lived in Kemnay and the air smelt exactly the same, of bored cows and pigs. But still we'd struggle wearily out of the tent, pack up and set off for another day of trudging up mountains or getting lost in forests.

Thinking about Dad – and Mum – brought a lump to my throat. Would I ever see them again? When the chickens first attacked, they went straight for the adults. In a matter of hours they were all gone, leaving us kids to fend for ourselves. I really missed my family. But I did not miss those camping trips.

The only thing that had made camping bearable was my older brother. Ethan loved it, every minute of it. In his mind he was preparing for when the world ended. He would point out high hills and say they'd be safe from floods, or talk about how aliens might not check out so far into the Grampian Mountains. One time he got really excited about this glen we found in the Cairngorms.

"We could house people over here," he said, pointing at a hut that looked half abandoned. "We're not that far from a road so we'd be able to bring in supplies. We could build a wall around the valley to keep wandering zombies out and then start planting vegetables. There's a lake a couple of miles over that way with fish we could eat and I'm sure there's deer and stuff we could hunt. Maybe we could even keep chickens."

Ha. If only he'd known. A few months later, chickens were keeping us. Real live chickens inside robotic suits, controlled by a signal that somehow increased their intelligence.

Ethan never told me if he had a plan for when giant robot chickens attacked our cities and enslaved us. So we'd had to come up with our own: by taking down their signal and freeing Aberdeen from the fowl menace. For like a week or so. The chickens found a way to get their signal working again and they came back in force. One or two at first then more and more as time went on. Each one hungry for more human prisoners. We'd managed to survive so far but it hadn't been easy. A lot of us had been taken. Little by little they were wearing us away. We had to do something to change that.

Although I hated camping, getting lost, muddy and tired, our trips with Dad had certainly come in handy these last few weeks.

I threw some more sticks on the fire and looked around. I was currently alone, stuck in a cave at the top of a hill, woods all around. I wasn't particularly worried about being found. From what I could see, the chickens' base wasn't that close to here and the cave should hide the fire pretty well. As for the smoke, I was using old, dry sticks so there wasn't much of it. A trick my brother had shown me.

I shook my head, trying to stop thinking of him. It didn't help and it only made me upset. I'd come to terms with his capture long ago. We were right in the middle of Aberdeen when I lost him, running away from a stalking Catcher on the first day the chickens attacked. I hadn't seen him since. It just made sense to assume he hadn't managed to get away. It hurt but at least I hadn't seen him taken. Not everyone was that lucky.

We needed everything we could get our hands on to defeat the chickens. Food, supplies, other children – they all helped. So while the chickens were still attacking in dribs and drabs, our scouting parties pushed out into the more remote areas of Aberdeen, looking for everything we could use. Every so often we came across groups, cut off from the rest of the city with no idea what was going on. Some didn't even know we'd managed to drive out the chickens for a while. These encounters usually went one of two ways.

Either the group would be delighted to find other kids and join us, or they'd throw stuff at us until we went away. We kept an eye on the throwers and it's depressing how many of them ended up in a chicken's gut.

The group we met at Bridge of Don had joined up easily. Their leader had recently left, and a string of bad luck with chickens had told them that they needed to find help fast. We took them, and their supplies of course, back into the centre of town. On the journey they talked about what they'd been through...

"Things went OK at first. We were left alone and managed to negotiate a truce with some of the other groups," one of the kids was saying, a girl with spiky, ginger hair. "Then one group started picking on the rest of us but they all got caught."

"So were you able to claw back what was lost?" I said brightly.

They just looked at me for a moment, then went back to talking. I guess maybe they hadn't got my joke so I started trying to think up a better one.

"Mostly we stayed where we were and tried to keep out of sight. But Ethan wasn't happy just sitting around. When the chickens didn't turn up for a while he took a team to investigate. Then a Catcher showed up two days later."

I stopped, my train of thought firmly derailed, and turned to look at her. "Ethan? Did you say *Ethan?*"

She looked at me weirdly. "Yeah, that's his name. Why?"

"Describe him."

"I said *why*?"

I might have lost my temper a little. The next thing I knew I was holding Hedgehog-head by the front of her jacket, like you'd see in some sort of crime movie. "*Describe him.*"

"Tall, over sixteen, blond hair, glasses, wore boots, had a long brown jacket, seemed sad..."

I must have made an impression because the words flooded out of her mouth in one long sentence. Then Rayna grabbed me and pulled me away.

"Jesse, what do you think you're doing?"

"She said Ethan. It might be my brother."

Rayna's eyes had narrowed. She was the only one I talked to about my brother. She knew enough to realise the description fit.

"Did he talk about zombies?" she asked the girl, who was looking at me with wide eyes. The girl had nodded, still staring at me.

"You're Jesse?" she said. "He thought you'd been captured right at the start."

Although I'd suspected Ethan had been taken during the very first attacks, somehow hearing that he'd been free all this time, and I'd missed him by just a few days, was hard to swallow.

That had been a bad day. But it had spurred me into action. My big brother was out there, fighting the chickens. There was a slim chance he was still free. I had to try and find him...

I thought I heard a sound outside my cave hideout and froze, one hand on my knife. It wouldn't have done any good against a Catcher but it felt reassuring in my grip. I stood poised for a minute but nothing else happened. Eventually I settled back down beside the fire.

Persuading the council to let me go on my own little mission had been... interesting.

"You want to do what?" Cody had spluttered, glaring at me.

"I heroically volunteer to scout out the land around the chickens' base for weak points that might be exploitable. The more we know about it the better chance we have to pull a trick on the fowl fiends and catch them with their tail feathers down."

"But what if you get captured? You might not come back!"

I grinned at him. "I'll just have to pluck up my courage."

"Do you even have a plan?"

"Not eggs-actly. But I'm not chicken, if that's what you think."

He sighed and paused for a moment. Cody had never warmed to my chicken jokes. "You know what? I like this plan. Either you come back with information or you never come back at all. How soon can you leave?"

So, two days after hearing news of my brother, I'd set out after him.

So far I hadn't had much luck. Ethan must have had at least a month's head start on me, maybe more. Dad had tried to teach me the basics of tracking but even if I'd been a master I doubt it would have done any good. So instead I'd been tracking back and forth across the country, going to places he'd mentioned in different end-of-the-world plans. This cave had been my last hope.

Suddenly I heard a rushing sound, like a plane in the distance. I leapt to my feet, recognising it as the sound of an approaching Catcher zooming somewhere at high speed. They went past every so often and had become part of life. When it didn't slow down I banked the fire and got into my sleeping bag. Tomorrow would be another day of searching, this time heading towards where the chickens seemed to have their base. I couldn't think of anywhere else he would be.

My walkie-talkie was inside my backpack, which I was using for a pillow. For a moment I was tempted to pull it out and call Rayna, but I resisted. It was the middle of the night and she was probably fast asleep.

I'd talk to her tomorrow.

CHAPTER 3

RAYNA: Aberdeen

It took ages to get to sleep. I spent most of the time staring at the ceiling, trying to forget what had happened that day. I must have dozed off at some point, though, because the next thing I knew the alarm was going off. I groaned and idly hit it to shut it up.

The sun must have just started rising because it was still fairly dark. The only light was a thin red line that stretched across the wall. I stared at it for a while, my brain not fully working yet. I was tempted to just lie there. Let the rest of the world take care of itself. Just stay in bed and sleep this reality away.

But I couldn't do that. So I heaved myself to my feet and started to get dressed.

At least I had my own room these days. The brief respite from chicken attacks following the Battle of Pittodrie had given us time to get properly organised and make a few safe havens in the city. Now that the chickens weren't such an immediate threat we didn't have to hide underground, so we moved into hotels instead.

We'd all mostly banded together out of a need to stay safe, and we'd set up a general council, which I had a seat on. But most kids still stuck with the groups they'd been in before. Not quite one big happy family. I still wasn't part of a group exactly. I tried to keep the peace and had picked up the nickname, the 'Ambassador'.

I spent most of my time with the Railway Gang, led by Noah. The hotel right next to the station had been transformed into council headquarters.

Jesse didn't belong to a gang these days either. I guess we'd formed one of our own, just him and me. When he wasn't off on solo missions, Jesse's room was next door to mine. We were close to the Brotherhood headquarters as well. One of our jobs was to keep an eye on them. When the chickens first attacked, a cult had formed called The Brotherhood of the Egg: a bunch of scared kids who worshipped the chicken overlords like gods. They dressed in chicken costumes and took on chickeny names. But the chickens just used them for information then betrayed them. Their leader Egbert was pecked up like a grain of corn, like all the other kids. Now they were just called the Brotherhood, and they were on our side – or so they said. But we needed to keep a close eye on them. I did it because my sister Hazel was their new leader. Jesse did it because they were the only ones who laughed at his jokes. That was just like Jesse. He...

I needed to stop thinking about Jesse. The longer we

went without hearing from him, the more I worried. If he never turned up again... I'm not sure what I would do. And there was a good chance of that.

At least I wouldn't see him be taken. That would be the worst thing I could possibly imagine.

I quickly got washed and dressed, then I left my room and turned down the corridor.

I found Noah in the communications room. When I'd first met him he was a scared kid, about my own age but a lot scrawnier. We'd all been forced to lose weight and swap fat for muscle. Noah had really manned up. He was still scrawny but much stronger and he wasn't as scared any more. Or at least he didn't show it. We had all learned to control our fear in the chicken apocalypse.

"Hey," he said, idly sipping a mug of tea. All around us computers were beeping and kids were tapping at keyboards. It was a confusing mishmash of technology, old and new. On one side of the room we had Apple Macs, looted from the nearby Apple store. On the other kids sat next to radios, listening intently with their headphones and twiddling knobs. In a corner was a bunch of TVs, some getting intermittent reception from TV channels worldwide, others tuned in to the chickens' own news channel. A chicken in a ridiculous hat flickered across one of the screens but I couldn't hear what it was saying.

Communication was important. We hadn't heard anything from the rest of the UK for a long time. I knew that the army had been smashed and the chickens had almost complete control. From the little we'd heard, Aberdeen was the only place that wasn't completely under chicken control. So we needed to know what was going on abroad. It gave us hope to know that the Americans and most of the rest of the world were still there, still fighting.

It was a shame they weren't winning.

"Hey," I replied. "What's going on? Anything new?"

Noah winced then nodded. "Poland's gone."

I felt my heart freeze. "All of it?"

"Yup." He took another sip from his mug. "The chief chicken broadcast a message a few hours ago. They completely surrendered. I think their army lost a big battle. Or maybe they just got tired of fighting. It's happened before."

"But they were the last ones left."

He sighed. "I know. That's Europe gone. The council are not going to be happy about that when I tell them."

"Shouldn't Glen tell the council? He's Head of Communication after all. It should be him."

Noah gave his twisted smile and shrug combo. "You know him. He doesn't like being anywhere near Cody."

"Can't really blame him." Someone handed me a mug of tea and I took it with thanks. A lot of us had started drinking tea lately. It cost a lot of electricity to heat the water but these days we had more than enough. One of the first things we did after the Battle of Pittodrie was to get a power station running again.

The Brotherhood, in an attempt to show they could be useful, had marched to the onshore control centre of the Aberdeen Bay Wind Farm to assess the situation. I'm not sure what they did – Jesse thought they just pressed buttons until things started happening – but the turbines started turning and we had power. It meant we could have light, heat and most gadgets, except our mobile phones. Getting electricity back, more than anything else, convinced a lot of people that we were strong enough to fight the chickens.

Even now, though, some people thought we were doing the wrong thing; that it would be safer to just give in. And it wasn't even the Brotherhood like you'd expect. They were watched very closely but seemed happy enough to be out from under the clawed foot of chicken oppression.

Glen came bustling over while the tea was working its magic. Unlike Noah he hadn't shed any of the excess weight he'd been carrying for as long as I knew him. Though since he spent most of his time in this room I suppose that wasn't a surprise.

"Noah, Ambassador." He nodded to me before getting right to the point. "There's a council meeting today, right?"

"Yes, Glen," Noah said wearily. We both knew where this was going.

Glen picked up on his tone. "You may be getting tired of this but it's important. If you could get the GPS satellite locator then we could send messages out as well as receiving them. We might even be able to contact the Allied army."

"I know, I know, but you've been asking about this for ages. Nothing's changed. You'll get the same answer," Noah replied.

"Even so, ask again. It's vital that we regain contact with the outside world. If they knew we were here..."

"...they'd launch an all-out rescue attempt, going deep into chicken territory, which they've not managed in any way, just to save a bunch of kids who are surviving on their own?" finished Noah. He raised an eyebrow. "Do you really think that will happen?"

Glen shrugged. "It's worth a shot."

"Yes it is," I said, before a fight could break out. "But getting the satellite locator would be a dangerous mission and it might attract unwanted attention. You know that."

"You made me Head of Communication. I'm just doing my job."

"So you'll tell the council about it in person?" Noah cut in.

"Noooo... I'm busy here." Glen looked about shiftily. "But you can ask for me."

"Fine," Noah said, resigned. "You'll need a miracle though."

"It's just important that you ask," Glen said, before walking back to his desk in front of a TV.

"Come on," Noah said, glancing at a watch. He reached behind him and grabbed a portable TV from the table. "We should go. The council meeting will start soon."

I groaned but straightened up from where I'd been leaning against a desk and followed him out the door. "What are we meeting about today?"

"The usual. Updates about what's been going on. They'll probably want a report from you about Jesse."

Yay. Sounded like a barrel of laughs.

CHAPTER 4

It was impossible for one person to be in charge of all the gangs that had sprung up around Aberdeen since the chickens first attacked, but we couldn't afford to be divided. So the council had formed, all the influential people in Aberdeen coming together to discuss how best to survive in this harsh new world.

Or at least that was the theory. What actually happened most of the time was a lot of arguing.

It would probably be like that today. When Noah and I arrived Cody was already there, Percy the ever-attentive shadow at his right hand. Cody was our strategist, working out how to survive in the long term. Sadly that seemed to make him think he was our leader. Today he'd taken his place at the head of the table as usual. He liked making displays of power. At first Noah had tried to fight him, getting there extra early, but now he'd given up. There was no point. He saved his energy for fighting Cody when they disagreed. Which was all the time.

Halfway down the table was Jeremy. I gave him a

wave and he grinned back at me. Jeremy was in charge of scouting and looking for supplies. The chickens had left some warehouses around the place, all stuffed with things to eat, but they couldn't last long. Jeremy and his team were in charge of going through the houses and shops in Aberdeen and collecting any tins or other lasting supplies. They weren't supposed to take anything else but I knew they did. I didn't like the stealing and others felt the same, but there wasn't much we could do about it. We needed that food and we couldn't watch everyone.

Next to Jeremy was Deborah, looking as if she wanted to be somewhere else. Her hair was tied back neatly and her well-scrubbed hands were fidgeting on the table. Deborah didn't like coming to meetings, feeling that she had better things to do. I agreed. After all she was our head doctor. Well, I say doctor. We didn't have doctors. But we did have kids whose parents had been doctors or who had wanted to be doctors. They spent all their time with a medical textbook in one hand and a dictionary in the other. They weren't professionals but everyone felt lucky to have them.

Sally sat across from Deborah, looking the complete opposite. Her face was covered with dirt and she pushed her scruffy hair out of her eyes with muddy fingers. She was staring into space and seemed disconnected from the world around her. But Sally might be the most important person at the table.

All our food came from scavenging and we knew this was a problem. Before the chickens attacked, Aberdeen had about quarter of a million citizens, most of them adults. We now had less than five hundred kids. While most of the fresh vegetables, meat, milk and juice had rotted away, there was enough stuff in tins lying around to last for a while. But not forever. Eventually the tins would run out and we'd starve. Some rationing was already in place. When the chickens were gone for a while, something had to be done.

Sally had come up with the solution. Like Jesse and myself she was one of the few kids who hadn't lived in Aberdeen before the attacks. She'd lived with her parents on a farm just outside the city. I don't know how she'd got here – not all kids were comfortable talking about 'That Day' – but I was glad she was with us. It had been her idea to start growing crops. She taught people how to dig up vegetable gardens and allotments. She dug over a nearby park, planting row after row of vegetable seeds and some fruit canes as well. We were all looking forward to the day we could have potatoes and carrots again.

My sister Hazel sat a bit apart from everyone else. Nobody really trusted the Brotherhood right now. When the chickens had been driven out of Aberdeen some of them had left and joined other groups but a solid core had stayed together. They kept themselves to themselves, mostly, hanging out in a big warehouse that they'd taken over down by the docks. They still wore white robes covered in feathers, though they'd got rid of the masks and the dinosaur slippers. There had been talk of throwing them out of Aberdeen or feeding them to the chickens but the council had put a stop to that. The fact of the matter was, we needed them. Without them we wouldn't have electricity, lasers, or a number of other useful devices that they made out of the wrecks of Catchers. So for the moment they stayed. But that didn't mean they were liked.

Hazel nodded at me when I came in, then went back to glaring at the last member of the council: Blake. Blake was dangerous. In theory I should like him. He was absolutely dedicated to fighting chickens. He excelled at it. And that was the problem. I'd once been that fanatical about beating the chickens. I'd gathered everyone together in a mad plan to defeat our enemy. And nearly everyone in Aberdeen had been caught because of it.

Then there was my other problem with Blake. He didn't fight chickens because he hated them, or because he felt driven to. He did it because he thought it was fun.

With the founding of the council Blake had found his role in life. He led and trained our army; what there was of it. He even had a special team that tracked down trouble and dealt with it. And he was very good at his job. I was happy he did it. I would just be happier if he did it a long, long way from me.

In some respects his job was similar to mine. He fought chickens; I fought to keep us all together. Whenever groups were arguing or we heard about another bunch of kids hiding away somewhere, I was sent to deal with it. I was also sent to deal with the Brotherhood when people stopped trusting them; the scavengers when they kept food for themselves; the communicators when they spent more time watching old movies than keeping an ear out for approaching Catchers; and the farmers when they got into arguments and started throwing mud around. Basically I was sent to deal with the most pressing problems of the day.

Hazel, Cody, Percy, Blake, Sally, Jeremy, Deborah, Noah, Glen and me: the team that stood between Aberdeen and the chickens.

Cody called the meeting to order, as usual. "Attention. Attention. Shall we begin?"

The room grew quiet and people turned to look at him. I took a seat and enjoyed the brief peace. I knew from experience that it wasn't likely to last long.

"Now, I think Noah has something to tell us. Noah?"

Noah nodded to Cody and stood, placing the TV on the table. He looked grim.

"Europe has fallen."

There was instant chaos at his words. People began yelling, some screaming. Cody banged on the table a few times with a judge's hammer, though I've no idea where he'd got it from.

"Let him finish. Then freak out," he said, and order was restored.

Noah took a deep breath and continued, "Poland surrendered early this morning. The chickens recorded it and their leader has been broadcasting it ever since."

The TV screen fuzzed for a moment then lit up. I could see the chickens' leader, known to us as King Cluck, glaring straight at the camera, just an ordinary cockerel wearing what looked like an upside-down colander on his head. Wires trailed around it, and lights flashed and blinked. Behind him was a flag, half white, half red. He'd be hilarious if he didn't keep taking over countries.

"People of the world. I know you can hear me." The voice was weird, seeming to come from everywhere at once. King Cluck's beak didn't ever move. He just stared at the screen.

"Poland has fallen and is ours. The following changes will be made. As it is now part of the glorious Chicken Empire the name of the capital will be changed from Warsaw to Warsquawk. The flag will also change appropriately. Red and white are not good colours." Behind him a new flag appeared, striped green and yellow. Briefly a picture flashed up, of a white bird on a red background wearing a crown. "The coat of arms is, however, acceptable.

"Now that we have Poland you must be wondering what we'll do next. The answer is Turkey. We will complete our long-term goal of conquering that country and renaming it Chicken. Because we are the superior bird and we will conquer the world!" King Cluck started cackling.

Noah reached forward and turned off the TV. "That chicken is crazy."

"Yeah, but he's beating us," Hazel chimed in.

Cody sighed. "Yes he is. What about resistance in other countries or cities? Are any of them fighting back?"

Noah shrugged. "We don't know. The truth is they could be and we just haven't heard anything. We sometimes intercept communications from big countries like America who have satellites, but we haven't recently. Of course if you want us to contact them we could try to get that thing Glen keeps asking about."

"The magic satellite whatsit that will solve all our problems?" Cody rolled his eyes. "The one that's miles away in Garthdee, an area we haven't even begun to explore yet, which is probably very dangerous? No, we're not going to get it. We need Glen. Every council member is too precious to risk, especially those who can't take care of themselves. Glen is our communications expert. If we lost him, what would we do?"

"Why can't someone else just go get it?" Sally spoke up.

"We don't know what it looks like," I told her. "Glen would have to come with us and it's quite far away."

"So why do we need it anyway? We're getting signals from America and Europe. Why can't we send them back?"

"From what Glen tells me it's not that easy." Noah

made a circular shape in the air with his hands. "Earth is a ball, right? Well we can only send signals in straight lines. To get them as far as America or somewhere we'd have to bounce the signals off satellites. To find the satellites we need that device."

"Which is too risky right now." Cody interrupted. "You can tell Glen – again – that he'll get the chance when we need it. Let's move on."

Noah winced, obviously not happy with Cody's decision but unwilling to fight him over it. He sat back down.

"Now, there was an attack yesterday. The foraging teams were hit and several people were abducted. We were well prepared, but our effort proved... inconclusive," said Cody.

I saw again Sam getting plucked into the air and heard the wails of his sister as I told her what had happened. She was probably still in her room sobbing. They'd only been back together for a few months but I could tell they were very close. We had to keep an eye on her. A few siblings and friends had given themselves up to the chickens after their loved ones were taken. They were so desperate to see them again.

"These attacks are getting more frequent but they're sending less experienced chickens, which are less of a danger," Cody continued. "That means—"

But we didn't get to find out what it meant, because that's when the giant robot chicken burst through the ceiling.

CHAPTER 5

There was a moment of shock where none of us reacted. I mean we were in the centre of Aberdeen here. We had lookouts and guards. There was no way a chicken should have been able to get that close without warning. But here it was.

Percy was the first to react. "Get down!" he yelled, leaping forward and pushing Cody out of the way. The chicken pecked down as he acted. Percy punched up at the giant creature but its beak hit him in the shoulder. Percy bounced off, flying away and crashing into the wall. Cody hit the floor and rolled under the table.

By this point the others were beginning to move. Most followed Cody's lead and dived beneath the table. Jeremy and Hazel ran towards the door, desperate to get away from that awful, grasping beak. I noticed that Blake had gone with them and I frowned. Maybe he wasn't as brave as I thought he was.

Well, if he didn't stop the intruder I'd have to.

"Hey, Featherface," I yelled, diving further into the

room, drawing my shock-stick as I went. "Come get some!"

"Get down, Rayna," Noah whispered from under the table, but I gestured for him to be quiet. The chicken had already seen me, but it didn't seem to have noticed them yet. I just had to distract it until the guards arrived – which should be any moment now.

The second invention the Brotherhood had made for us, after the big lasers, were shock-sticks. They were exactly like they sounded: long staffs that emitted an electric shock when they hit something. They were created to help us fight Commandos: just bigger than life-size robot chickens. They wouldn't do anything to a huge Catcher. Nothing but get its attention. And that was exactly what the people under the table needed me to do.

The Catcher was stuck. The room we were in was partly underground, so it had smashed straight in from above. Its body and head were dangling into the room, but its huge wings were trapped on the floor above. It lashed razor-sharp claws as its head lurched towards me, pecking viciously. It shouldn't be able to stay there for much longer. The guards surrounding the building must already have noticed something was wrong, but as long as the giant chicken was in this confined space it was a danger to everyone. And we wouldn't be able to deal with it as effectively if it had a kid inside it.

I hit it with the stick and watched the current flow

through it. That certainly got its attention. Hopefully it would see me as more of a threat.

Its eyes glowed briefly red, though it didn't fire its laser, and it turned towards me, enraged.

I hit it again then hopped to the side as it snapped in my direction. I'd hoped to be able to just back out the door, but there was stuff in my way so I squashed up against the wall.

"What's the matter, a bit too plump?" I groaned. Then I had to dart away sharpish as it tried to hurl itself after me. It pushed further into the room, causing plaster to rain from the ceiling and thump against the table. I heard squealing from beneath.

So did the chicken. It turned its attention back to those trapped below and I had to jump in and smack it again. It snaked its neck at me and I spun to one side then hit it several more times.

Surely it wouldn't be long now before the guards came running?

Percy began scrambling to his feet, groaning. The chicken must have knocked him dizzy because he looked wobbly and didn't seem to know where he was – or that there was a giant chicken just behind him.

The chicken heard the groan and turned back, snapping at him.

I did the only thing I could. I dived across the table, sliding on the slick wood, and got to the two of them just in time. I flung out my arm before me and somehow managed to wedge the shock-stick in the chicken's mouth. It looked surprised for a moment then jerked its head sharply.

I fell back, knocking Percy down with me. The chicken looked at me steadily for a moment, enjoying the power it had. Then it slowly and methodically closed its mouth, snapping the stick in two.

I could only watch, helpless, as it bent down towards me, beak gaping wider and wider.

This was it. After all the months of fighting, after all the effort and pain I'd gone through, it was going to end like this. Just one small scuffle in a hotel basement. I would be pecked up like an insect and taken to serve the chicken masters for the rest of my days.

The last thought as that gaping maw engulfed me was that I might see Jesse again.

Then there was a sharp twanging sound and the chicken's neck exploded.

Part of it just disappeared, like paper in a flame. The chicken whipped itself back up, almost losing its head in the process. I could see the exposed chute that kids would slide down when they got pecked up.

The chicken scrabbled to get out of there but now its size worked against it, and it gradually disintegrated as it writhed about. When it finally hauled itself out of the room it was riddled with holes, showing the exposed insides. It jumped up with a relieved squawk but a red laser followed it out of the hole, hitting it right in the rear jets. There was a thump up above as it finally keeled over, defeated.

With a groan I got to my feet, pulling Percy up with me.

Standing in the door, laser in hand and a smug, self-satisfied look on his face, was Blake.

"Just like a duck hunt," he said, blowing some smoke from the barrel of his weapon.

"Thanks," I said grudgingly. "You took your time though."

If anything his grin got wider. "I had to wait for it to charge," he told me. "Otherwise I'd have been happy to shoot it sooner."

Now wasn't the time to gloat. "We need to get everyone out of here," I told him. His grin faded somewhat and he nodded.

He leaned out the door and yelled a few things, probably summoning people from further in the building. I sat Percy down in a chair and made sure everyone under the table was safe. They were. Not happy but safe. Jeremy and Hazel didn't come back in but some of Deborah's medics did.

"Great job," Noah said to me. "We all owe you one, Rayna."

"We've got to discuss what just happened," barked Cody, getting straight back to business.

I looked up from where I was sitting in a chair, having Deborah look over me. Cody was standing next to Percy while a doctor assessed him. They said he'd be fine after a rest, but I got the feeling Cody was really worried for his bodyguard and second in command.

"We know what just happened. We almost got eaten

by a chicken," said Blake. Cody shot him one single, piercing glare and the adventurer quietened down.

"Yes, I got that. I was there. But how did it get in here to attack the council in the first place?"

We were silent for a while, considering his point.

"Not just attack the council, it tried to get you first," I said.

Cody looked at me, still in control, and raised one eyebrow. "What do you mean?" he asked.

"It attacked the person sitting at the head of the table. Everyone else sits in random places at every meeting but you always sit at the head. You're well known for it." By well known I meant that probably everyone had complained about it at one point or another. Cody knew but he didn't comment.

"That could just be coincidence," he said, still calm, still in control. "But it definitely took on the council. Which proves one thing: we've got to do something about our defences."

He was right. We all knew he was right. The chicken wouldn't just randomly attack an underground room in a central hotel. It must have known we'd be there. We had been targeted.

Everyone else seemed too stunned by the sudden attack to contribute anything to the discussion. Cody looked at them in disgust and motioned Blake and me off to one side.

"You two haven't worked together before, right?" he said in a low voice.

"That's right," Blake confirmed. I merely nodded.

"Then here's how it goes. Blake, you work out ways to beef up our defences. I don't want anything like this happening again. This hotel is our home right now and I won't stand for a chicken getting this close to it. Rayna, talk to everyone you can. I want to know who slipped up and let the Catcher get this close. Got it?"

I rocked back on my feet, surprised at the vehemence in his voice. Cody was angry, properly angry. That was never good.

"Where should I start?" I asked, trying to be professional. With Cody in this state it wouldn't do any good to say that I didn't want to work with Blake.

"Go have a word with your sister."

He turned and, without one more word, walked back to where Percy was still sitting. Hunkering down in front of him he passed the black-haired lieutenant a bottle of water and helped him drink it.

I turned away. Cody was right. The chicken should never have got this close to us. It just confirmed what I'd been suspecting for a while.

One of us was a traitor.

CHAPTER 6

"Noah, wait up." I saw him walking back towards the train station, where a lot of his gang still hung out. He turned and flashed me a smile.

"Rayna, thanks again for everything in there. That was really quick thinking on your part."

"Blake probably had it handled." I brushed off his praise but smiled inside. Noah had a talent for making people feel pleased with themselves. "I just wanted to talk with you a bit, get an idea of what you thought of the attack."

"You mean about the spy?"

I nodded. I'd told Noah about my fears a few weeks ago. It had been worrying when he hadn't just laughed and called me paranoid.

It began with small things at first. Chickens appeared unexpectedly when we were on undercover missions; a few secret outlying groups got picked off; people travelling under cover of darkness got jumped. But it was happening more and more often.

I couldn't imagine who would do such a thing. And

I didn't even like thinking about it. But I had to accept the fact that someone was telling the chickens vital information about us.

"There's no way the chickens could have known we'd be in there," I said, lowering my voice. "Someone must have told them."

"Any idea who it could be?" he said.

I shook my head. "Someone who knows a lot of information. The attacks are too accurate, too often. I..."

Noah shook his head slightly, his eyes flicking back over my shoulder. I turned to see Sally approaching.

"Hi." She smiled at us. "Thank you so much, Rayna, for protecting us from the Catcher."

"Oh, it was no problem." I looked at Noah uncomfortably while he grinned back.

"No, it was very brave. I just froze up. I don't think I could stand up to one of them like you do."

"Well, you know..." I really didn't like getting praise for fighting chickens. All I'd done was hit it a few times. Blake had been the one with the big gun. "We've all got our jobs. You grow potatoes and I deal with problems like that."

"Yes, I suppose you're right." She paused and stared up at the blue sky. "It's a lovely day today. Really beautiful for late summer."

Sally was kind but I found her polite chitchat very tiring. "Sorry to be rude, Sally, but I need to go and get a new shock-stick."

"I've got work to do as well. Bye Rayna, bye Noah."

She waved her hands airily and floated off. We looked after her for a second.

"You'd expect gardeners to be more down to earth," I said.

"Oh, hush. She's a nice person."

"I know. She's just so... happy." I looked at my watch and then back at Noah. "I really had better be off. I'll talk to you later?"

"Definitely. Take care. And play nice with your sister."

"Only if she plays nice with me," I muttered and stalked off.

I found Hazel where I expected to, back at the hotel entrance, preparing to clean up the mess Blake had made of the chicken. To find her, I just had to follow the sound of revving engines.

The Brotherhood needed supplies to make our weapons. Apparently the chickens had planned to set up a Catcher factory in Aberdeen and ship them off to wherever they were needed around the world, but we'd driven them out before that could happen. We'd been using the tools and materials they'd left behind, but now that they were running out we used everything we could from the wrecked remains of Catchers. So whenever we managed to down one, Hazel and some other Brotherhood members drove up on quad bikes and dragged them back to their warehouse.

Today she was working with a kid called Kyle, who was Jeremy's second in command. I was fairly sure Kyle actually ran everything important. He was the one who made sure supplies went where they needed to be. He catalogued what the scavenging teams brought back. Jeremy led the teams but ultimately Kyle did all the important work. I hadn't seen much of him before the Battle of Pittodrie but from what I'd heard, he'd spent most of his time with one of the groups that moved about Aberdeen, scuttling from one house to another. It wasn't an easy way to live and he'd picked up a nervous attitude.

I walked up to them and waved. "Hey, you got a minute?"

Kyle jumped in his saddle and looked about as Hazel turned off her engine and gave me a big grin. "Hey, well done in there, sis. It was good work. What do you want to talk about?"

"Can I get another shock-stick?" I asked Kyle, holding up the broken pieces of my old one. "The Catcher broke mine."

He took the two halves in his hands and glared at them. "These don't grow on trees, you know. We don't have enough for you to keep breaking them."

"I know but it was an emergency. And I need a new one."

He rolled his eyes. "Whatever. Anything for a council member, I guess. I'll grab you one after I've finished helping Hazel."

"Could you go and get it now, *please*?" I asked, putting a special emphasis on the please. "I'll wait here with Hazel."

He glanced at me, suddenly uncertain, then nodded and scuttled off. Hazel strode into the hotel towards the Catcher's remains, her smile shrinking. I followed.

"It's business then, is it?" she asked as we walked towards the large hole in the floor.

"Yeah, it is. I've got a few questions."

"Because of the attack? Or has something else happened you want to pin on us?"

My heart sank. She was already getting annoyed. I tried to keep the peace.

"Look, I just want to ask you one or two things, that's all. It'll be over quickly and then you can get back to work."

"Work, work, work. That's all it is with you. Why can't we ever talk about something else?"

"Well, what do you want to talk about?"

"How's Jesse getting on?"

I wasn't aware of doing anything, but my body language must have given me away because her face fell.

"Well, don't worry about it," she said after a moment. "He's sure to call soon. The chickens won't have got him yet."

"You know a lot about the chickens."

Hazel hesitated for a split second before shrugging. "You hang out with them for a few months, you tend to pick things up."

"A lot of stuff to pick up. That Jesse's still free, that there's a spy…"

Hazel had confirmed my suspicion that there was a traitor in Aberdeen. I don't know how she knew, but she'd taken me aside at a meeting last week and mentioned it. Sadly she could only tell us that a spy existed, not who it was. Which was kind of suspicious.

Hazel's eyes narrowed. Looks like, after a brief few pleasant words, we were back to fighting. "A spy I told you about immediately."

I rubbed my forehead. "Look, Hazel, I trust you. You know I do."

"Then why are you always going on at me like this? It's always 'Oh Hazel, have you sold us out to the chickens yet?' That's not trusting."

Something snapped inside me. "I said I trusted *you*. *Only* you. *Not* the Brotherhood."

Hazel gave a wild laugh. "So you think I'd just be going along with them if they were traitors? That I wouldn't turn them in? What would be the point? We were on the same side as the chickens once before and look how that worked out. We're with *you* now. You guys just aren't with *us*."

"What do you expect? You worked with the enemy. Egbert betrayed us and fed us all to his masters."

"And he's gone! No one's seen him since the Battle at Pittodrie. The Brotherhood's changed. We're working with you now. And things would go a lot smoother if you worked with us."

I took a few deep, calming breaths. Every time I tried talking to Hazel about this, we ended up getting in a fight. "Look, I'm sorry for the way you're being treated. But there's nothing I can do about that. Right now I just have to do my job and make sure the council is safe. Now, did you know about that attack beforehand? And did you tell anyone about where the council meeting would be held?"

"No and no."

"And you don't know who the spy is?"

"Nope. There is *something* you should know though."

I felt my pulse increase. This sounded serious. "What is it?" I asked.

But she didn't answer. Like Noah a minute ago she looked over my shoulder. "Hello, Blake."

"Hello," said a voice right in my ear.

I jumped, spinning round. Blake was standing there, leaning on his shock-stick. He was looking at the Catcher lying on the ground.

"Don't do that," I snapped at him.

He didn't seem too concerned, just grinned at me.

"Did you want anything?" I asked.

"Just checking in. Cody told me to check possible defensive weaknesses so that's why I'm here."

"To look at the big hole in the floor?" I glared at him.

He looked straight at Hazel, who flushed, and said, "Or the thing that caused it."

I opened my mouth, about to tell him to back away from my sister, but Hazel had obviously had enough.

"I've told you everything I can. I've got to get this Catcher back to our warehouse. See you at the next council meeting."

Just then Kyle hurried up with my new shock-stick, which I snatched from him before shooing him away. "Can you at least tell me where you're getting your information?" I whispered to Hazel.

But Hazel and a now very angry Kyle were busy attaching chains to the Catcher's suit. They pulled them tight then stormed off towards the quad bikes.

"Wait," I called after her.

She looked me dead in the eyes. "Trust us first," she told me. "Then we'll trust you."

They hooked the chains on to their quad bikes and revved the engines. I watched as the Catcher was wrenched out of the hole, through the hotel door and off down the street, clattering along.

I stared after them. Part of me wanted to follow them, hug my sister and apologise for fighting with her. But I just couldn't. I'd hated the Brotherhood for so long, it felt like a constant weight on my shoulders. No matter what I did I couldn't seem to drop it.

I rounded on Blake, who was watching them leave, looking satisfied. "What was that for?"

"I don't trust them. They keep trying to duck out of things."

"We need them on our side; you can't just go insulting them like that. What's your problem?"

He seemed about to answer me when one of his soldiers ran up. "Blake, Blake," she yelled.

He focused on her immediately. "What is it?" he asked.

"You've got to come quickly. There's trouble at the farms. Three Catchers."

I looked at Blake and felt my eyes widen. "That's where Sally was going," I told him.

He cursed and turned, sprinting off. "Get Cody to send some more backup," he yelled over his shoulder. Then he grabbed the whistle that hung around his neck and gave it a swift, ringing peep.

His group materialised around him, as if they'd been waiting for his call. They were always nearby, the most experienced chicken hunters we had. They started running towards the farms. I sprinted after them and quickly caught up.

"What are you doing?" Blake yelled at me.

"I need to see this," I yelled back. "First the attack this morning and now this? Right where Sally is?"

"Do you think they're trying to get more council members?"

"Well, we won't know until we get there," I yelled at him, accelerating. "Come on!"

CHAPTER 7

It was a hard run to the farms, along College Street before turning on to Wellington Place. Sally had needed an area of grass or earth to farm but the centre of Aberdeen was mostly tarmac and granite. So she'd settled on the Bon Accord Terrace Gardens. They weren't very big but they were very central. If those farms worked well, she talked about developing Duthie Park, like they had during World War Two.

When we got there everything was in chaos. Sally's farmers were running all over the place, pursued by the three Catchers. Sally, meanwhile, was trying to attack a Catcher with a shovel, screaming with rage at the top of her voice. I stopped when I saw her, surprised. She was normally so calm. Then I saw her plants, the rows of crops that she'd been working so hard on. Several of them had been squashed flat by big chicken claw-prints. I guess seeing all her work trampled had snapped something deep inside her.

However brave it might have seemed to attack a Catcher like that, it was also dumb. No human could take on a Catcher with just a shovel. From what we'd learned via TV and radio, Catchers were even bulletproof. That's why we preferred lasers.

But the lasers had one distinct weakness. They consumed a lot of energy, and I mean a lot. They guzzled more energy than a toddler on sugar. We needed to plug them into the mains or hotwire them into a car, which was dangerous. The Brotherhood was working on some portable ones but they would take a while to develop. So if we brought lasers to a fight, they had to be set up ahead of time, like the ambush I'd helped with yesterday.

If we didn't have lasers then things got tricky.

"Nets," I snapped at Blake as we started running forward.

"You don't have to tell me," he replied calmly.

I'd seen it before, in him and a few of his crew. When trouble started they didn't freak out like some did. They calmly assessed the situation and then acted. I guess some people just handle danger better than others.

"Angus, Connie, you take the one on the right. Andrea, Stuart, the one on the left. The one in the middle is mine. Everyone else, get people out of here."

I joined Blake as he ran towards his Catcher, which was beginning to stalk Sally. This wasn't going to be easy. Jesse and I were the first to take down a Catcher 'unarmed' but we'd had to pull a house down on it. Since then we'd come up with an easier, though much more risky, approach.

"Do you want to be bait or shall I?" I asked Blake, running beside him. He grinned.

"You can have the fun," he said, without even a hint of irony. 'Fun' was not the word I'd choose.

I pulled out my shock-stick as I ran, clanging it off the chicken's legs. Shock-sticks always got their attention. The chickens didn't seem to know what they were, and anyone carrying one was identified as a threat. The Catcher turned away from Sally and moved towards me. A brief strike to its neck and I dodged out of the way.

It buffeted me with its wing, throwing me backwards through the air. I landed with a thump on the hard ground. This wasn't a new Catcher like some of the ones we'd faced recently. Both the skill with which it controlled its machine and how plain it was, just a round body on legs without ornamentation, told me this was an old and experienced pilot. I worried for a second. Maybe this tactic wouldn't work.

I lay still, unable to get up, as the chicken approached me. I could hear screams and clanging all around. My shock-stick lay a few metres away, dropped as I landed. I rolled over onto my front and began to crawl for it, but I knew I wouldn't reach it in time.

The shadow of the bird descended on me.

I rolled over again. I wanted to see this part. I wanted to see it trying to eat me.

"Just try it," I snarled up at him. "I might be a bit more than you can swallow."

It bent over slowly, looking at me with something like curiosity; like it didn't know what to make of me. Its beak opened slowly, almost as if it was gently yawning. But what came next wouldn't be gentle. I'd seen it enough times to know. It would flash forward, its beak sinking deep into the soil. The jaws would snap shut then I'd be sent tumbling with a load of earth and seedlings down into the bowels of its stomach.

I glanced sideways, to make sure my timing was perfect. The other two Catchers lay still. They'd already been dealt with.

My Catcher seemed to notice this at the same time I did. It stopped moving, its eyes frantically revolving in their sockets with tiny squeaking noises. But it saw the trap coming far too late.

Blake sprinted out from where he'd been hiding beneath one of the defeated Catchers, next to the suddenly calm Sally. He slid on his knees when he got to me, like a striker after scoring a spectacular goal. His hand arched up and over, the net he'd been holding there unfolding gracefully. It spread through the air and came down over the Catcher's head.

And that was it. When I'd first tried out the nets I'd expected a few sparks, maybe a thump or something. But no. Without a fanfare the chicken's signal was cut off and it became just another useless lump of metal.

"He shoots, he scores!" Blake crowed, getting to his feet and dancing around with his arms in the air.

I breathed out sharply before hauling myself to my feet. "You took your time," I told him.

"You were such good bait. I was enjoying your performance."

"Well next time enjoy it less and act quicker."

"Alright. Though I don't know why you were worried. That was pretty easy."

"Yes. It *was* easy..." I frowned. "Blake, get your people over here right now."

"Why?" he asked, though he was sensible enough to begin beckoning them over before I answered his question. The farmers had already left and just us and Sally remained.

"Because that was easy. *Too* easy. The chicken piloting this thing was good. Too good to fall for something we've done so many times. Look at these Catchers. They're so basic. And look – there are dents from bullets and stuff. We shouldn't have been able to take them down so quickly."

"Which means..." Blake's eyes narrowed as he got it too "...that wasn't an attack."

"It was a diversion." I nodded, as a scream, quickly silenced, sliced through the air.

"That was Benny," Blake said. "It came from over there."

We moved as one in the direction of the scream, Sally still clutching her trusty shovel. When we got there we found a crumpled body beside a bush. Benny lay still, not moving.

"Is he alright?" someone asked, but Sally was already rushing forward. She bent down beside him, smoothing back his hair and checking his pulse.

"He's breathing normally," she told us, the confidence in her voice reassuring. "But he's unconscious. I don't know what could have cause—"

Sally was cut off by a second scream as something enormous, black and chicken-shaped burst from the bushes beside her. It was on to her in a second, moving oddly. Parts of it seemed to open up and flow over her, sucking her into its cavernous gut. She was dragged backwards into the bush, which rustled a few times and was still.

A second after getting over our shock we tore in after her, brushing leaves and twigs away from our faces.

"Sally!" I yelled. "Sally!"

"What happened? What was that?"

"I don't know, Blake. But make sure it doesn't get away with Sally."

We hunted around for a while, calling her name, but we all knew it was no good.

Sally had been taken.

We finally made our way back to the main battleground and found the Catchers also gone. Our nets lay shredded on the ground. Beside them was a single black feather.

Ever since the beginning of the chicken apocalypse I don't think I'd ever felt so defeated.

I looked at Blake and saw that he was feeling the same way. "What was that?" he asked.

I could only shrug. I didn't know.

CHAPTER 8

"So you have no idea what that thing was? It's an egg-nigma?"

I lay on my bed and stared at the ceiling. My walkie-talkie was sitting on my bedside table, Jesse's voice floating through it. He'd finally got round to calling me and I'd just finished filling him in on the attacks that day.

"Nope," I said. "I think Hazel might have an idea but she's not told me yet – because Blake was there."

"Shame they didn't eat him as well." Jesse didn't really know Blake. He'd been banned from council meetings since he make some joke about Cody trying to 'rule the roost'. But he knew how I felt about Blake.

"We need him," I reminded Jesse quietly, though privately I agreed. "The longer we have him the more effective we'll be."

"Unless he's the spy."

Now *there* was something I didn't want to think about. We knew it had to be someone on the council, but Blake was too useful. I hoped it wasn't him.

"Who do you think it is?" I asked.

"Well, I..." Jesse's voice cut off for a couple of minutes. Then it was back, though fuzzy with static. "Sorry, a chicken just flew over. Didn't want to risk it landing or anything."

My heart rate settled back to normal. "Where are you, anyway?"

"Just scouting out the chickens' base."

"What?" I sat bolt upright in bed. "Why are you talking to me while doing that?"

"Relax." Jesse's voice sounded almost sleepy. "I'm miles away, looking at it through binoculars. I'll see anything coming before it gets to me, and I'll hide. Besides, it's best to do this at night. I'm harder to see."

"What does it look like?"

"A huge barn – almost the size of an aircraft hangar – all big and red. They must have built it from scratch."

I lay back down. "Well, where is it? How easy is it to get to?"

His voice went quiet, though his tone stayed the same. "Not that easy. They've built it right by Kemnay."

"Your hometown? That's lucky."

"Not that lucky." Jesse sounded a bit bitter. "They're out in the country, miles from anywhere that isn't a farm, and it looks like they've levelled a fair amount of the village so there's no chance of hiding there. It's improved the place but it's still annoying. They've got a big fence round the barn that's probably electric. Half of the site is bordered by the River Don. I mean it isn't a big river but it'll be tricky to cross without our weapons getting soaked. So it'll be hard to attack and even harder to sneak anyone out."

"Sounds a pain."

"I don't know," Jesse said musingly. "With the right plan it should be doable..." He tailed off.

"Jesse," I told him sternly, "do *not* try and take that place on by yourself. Just find out what you can and get back here."

"Sure, sure."

"I mean it."

"Alright, alright. I'm not stupid."

I wasn't convinced. Great. More reason to worry.

"So, anyway. Traitors?" I diverted our conversation back to where we'd begun.

"Yeah, sorry." There was a pause for a moment, as if he was looking at notes. "Well, it has to be someone in the council. No one else should know all the information they're using to get to us. They're hitting too many supply runs, finding too many hidden bases. So that's you, Blake, Noah, Cody, Glen, Hazel, Deborah, Jeremy and Percy, I guess. It's not Sally, we know that much. We know it's not you. Glen isn't at any council meetings. I really doubt it'd be Noah."

"That still leaves us with six people. You don't really think it would be Cody, do you?"

"You never know," Jesse replied. "Cody could be a dove."

I stared silently at the ceiling above me. I knew Jesse was trying to make some sort of dumb joke but I couldn't figure out where he was going with it.

"OK," I said, eventually giving in, "get it over with. Why would he be a dove?"

"Because he could be planning to stage a coup."

If he was expecting laughter he was disappointed. All he got from me was stony silence. One thing I didn't miss about Jesse were his terrible jokes.

"You know," he continued, "it means a military takeover. And it's pronounced the same as the sound a dove makes. Actually, it's spelt oddly and before I knew how to pronounce it I was going to make a joke about—"

"You know, I'm really regretting getting you that dictionary. I thought your jokes would get better, not worse."

"It's one of the best gifts I've ever had," Jesse said, then his voice turned serious: "Really, though, watch out for Cody. This might be a way for him to gain control over Aberdeen."

"You seriously think Cody would work with the chickens to gain more power?"

"He didn't want to fight them to begin with, remember? He said it would draw unwelcome attention and that he'd get more done staying out of their way. It's not hard to imagine him working with them to get what he wants."

"But he was targeted today," I argued.

"Yeah, right before the much more successful attack on Sally. The one that actually worked."

Jesse was right, though I didn't like it. If Cody was the traitor, then we were in big trouble.

"So basically we can't trust anyone that's not you, me, Glen or Noah?"

"You can trust Hazel. She's your sister; she wouldn't betray you."

I wanted to believe him. But I just kept picturing her wearing the feathery Brotherhood uniform, arguing with me about fighting the chickens. I still couldn't trust my own sister.

I punched the wall, hard enough for Jesse to hear the thump. If he had, he didn't comment. "So what can we do now?" I asked.

There was a crackling of static through the radio. Maybe Jesse was eating something. I could picture him sitting there, bar of chocolate in hand, staring at the far-off barn and thinking.

"What you need is some way of narrowing down the suspects. Tell each of them something secret and see who reacts. But that could take ages and you couldn't be sure they wouldn't pass the information on to other people."

I felt something tingle at the back of my brain. "Not if we did it with a specific mission. Something the chickens would want to stop. We could tell different people different information about the mission and see which information gets passed on to the chickens – that would tell us who blabbed."

There was a pause, then Jesse replied, excited, "Yeah, that would work. But what mission?"

I grinned into the darkness. "I know just the thing."

CHAPTER 9

JESSE: Operation Henhouse Hustle

It really sucked being so far away from Rayna and not being able to chat easily. That was something I'd never really appreciated before the chicken apocalypse. Before if I wanted to talk to someone I could just message them on Facebook or text them. They could live hundreds of miles away and it wouldn't really matter.

Now I could only call Rayna on the radio and I didn't want to do that too often in case it was intercepted, which is why I'd asked her not to contact me. Also, she was always busy with something and I was probably annoying her. During the last few days I'd been sleeping during the day and sneaking about at night. Which meant that when I actually wanted to talk to Rayna she was usually asleep. And it was rarely a good idea to talk while sneaking around. The only reason I got away with it now was the distance between me and the chickens' barn.

As the light from the coming dawn started brightening the horizon I put down my binoculars and stretched my shoulders. On the dew-soaked grass beside me lay my notebook, slightly damp. I picked it up and settled it in my backpack, preparing to start the hour-long hike back to the farmhouse I'd been camping in. It was a bit annoying having to walk so far every night, but sleeping in a real bed was worth it.

It hadn't been hard to track down the chickens' headquarters. I just followed a few Catchers as they flew overhead, making sure I stayed out of sight. I'd probably learned everything I could from scoping the place out under cover of darkness; there wasn't much activity around the barn at night. But it helped to work out the general layout of the place. Maybe I'd go back in daylight, just once, and see what it looked like when everyone was awake, how well guarded the place seemed. Then it'd be time to head back to Aberdeen and make some plans. I already had a couple itching away at the back of my head but it all depended on finding the spy. I'd agreed to call Rayna tomorrow evening, once she'd completed her first spy-catching mission. Then we'd—

There was a noise, off to my left. A soft thud. I'd almost missed it but part of my mind was hyper alert and yelled at me to get down. I froze, peering through the leaves ahead of me.

There it was, a Catcher, the growing light of dawn glinting off its bronze exterior. It walked carefully, picking its way, barely making a sound. Its head swivelled left and right, scanning the road ahead.

I hadn't seen any patrols up until now. I wondered if it was again the work of this mysterious spy, putting the chickens on high alert. It was only an idle thought, a small whispering at the back of my mind, as I stared intently at the Catcher. It didn't seem to be in a hurry, moving slowly and carefully, making sure it missed nothing. It was between me and the farmhouse. If I tried to get past it, it would see me.

This wasn't good. I couldn't just wait it out. Dawn would be here soon and the chicken would easily be able to spot me. I could try and fight it but I didn't even have a shock-stick. I did have some of the Brotherhood's egg grenades, but it was more difficult to take out a chicken with one of those than you'd think. And even if I did somehow manage to take it down, I would alert every other Catcher in the area to my whereabouts.

Part of me was fleetingly tempted to just let the Catcher take me. The barn looked kind of nice in a basic way, and maybe my brother was inside.

Wait. I felt a grin creep across my face, like the light gradually flooding across the land. I had a plan.

I quickly slipped off my backpack and set it on the ground beside me. Then I started pulling stuff from my pockets, anything I didn't want the chickens to get, stuffing them inside the backpack. The bag was supposed to be waterproof. The notebooks and stuff would be fine. As I worked I thought quickly over my plan, made at the last moment and probably doomed to failure. Rayna would hate it; I knew that. But it was a risk I was willing to take. After all, I thought as I stuffed the walkie-talkie into my backpack, if everything went wrong I wouldn't be around for her to get mad at.

I crammed the bag under a bush and looked at the Catcher. It must have heard the leaves rustling because it straightened up, looking more alert than a moment ago. I crawled to the left and my hand found a large stone. The Catcher's head swivelled abruptly and it glared right at me. It knew where I was.

Time to get started.

I stood up and hurled the rock with all my might. It whooshed through the air and hit the chicken on the beak with a faint clang.

"Hey, Beaky!" I called out. "Want to hear a joke?"

CHAPTER 10

RAYNA: Aberdeen

I'd been planning in my head since speaking to Jesse. By the time Noah turned up at the communications room, Glen was on board. Noah was a harder sell. It had taken the better part of an hour, with Glen backing me up, before he'd agreed.

"You don't really need my permission anyway," he grumbled. "I don't have any control over Glen and I certainly don't have any control over you."

"True," I said, smiling at him, "but it wouldn't feel right doing this without your OK." I turned and walked towards the door.

"I think it's a big risk," Noah called after me. "Be very, very careful, Rayna."

"I will," I called back cheerily. Then I was out the door, on the way to put my plan into action.

I headed to the hospital and bumped into Cody on the way. He was striding towards his office. "Hey, Cody!" I called after him as he disappeared down a corridor. "Wait up."

I thought I heard him sigh, but he did stop.

"How's Percy doing?" I asked as I jogged up to him.

A faint blush of colour crept across his cheeks, though his expression didn't change at all. "He'll be fine," he told me. "Deborah says he has to stay in hospital a while longer, just to make sure he doesn't have a concussion or anything. But he should be out by tomorrow evening."

"That's great," I said enthusiastically.

"Hmmm..." Cody said noncommittally. "You want something. Now what is it?"

I stopped being jolly, which was a bit of a relief, and looked at him seriously. "What's the plan?" I asked him. "The long-term one? How do we beat them?"

He laughed. "The plan? We survive as long as possible. You know that."

"No, seriously. There's always another level with you. So what's *your* plan?"

He looked around then took my arm and guided me towards his office. "Come see this," he said.

Cody had commandeered one of the conference rooms in the hotel and turned it into his own personal office. He had maps tacked to the walls, stacks and stacks of notes from who knows where, and a computer hummed in a corner. Jesse thought all he did was play Minesweeper when no one was looking. He could have been right.

"Look at this," Cody said, closing the door behind me. The curtains were pulled tightly shut on the windows, only the electric lights showed anything. I looked at what he was showing me: a graph drawn on a piece of squared paper. I could make out a couple of lines, the boldest going steadily down.

"This charts how fast we're losing people," he told me. "At the rate we're going everyone will have been taken within the next year."

I looked at it, shocked. "That can't be right," I said. "We win a lot of the major engagements. People are mostly able to wander about freely. The scavenging teams are only hit about once a week."

"It doesn't matter," he told me honestly. "There aren't that many of us – two hundred, maybe three? I mean that's a lot when you gather us all together but there are just so many more chickens. They grab a few of us at a time, we take out a few of them. But they've got the numbers to spare and we frankly don't."

"A year." I looked at the red line, dipping steadily down. "We only have a year before all this collapses?"

He snorted, apparently amused. "Oh no, we've got much less time than that. Maybe six months?"

"What? What happens in six months? Why not a year?"

He pointed at the graph. "See that line there? That's where I think panic will set in. Once we lose half our numbers, people will start to freak out. They'll lose faith in the system, everyone working together. They'll start splitting off, each group leaving to look for a safer place. And Aberdeen will go back to the way it was. Only there'll be a lot fewer of us."

"What?" I looked at him, honestly bewildered. "But they can't think that. I mean, look at everything we've got now. Why would people give up like that?"

He shrugged. "They wouldn't be wrong. I've been trying to gather some information and from what people tell me, Catchers were taking fewer people when everyone was split apart and in hiding. There was a ton of food lying around so no one really went hungry. The only thing that is truly better now is that we've got electricity. And soon that won't be enough."

"Six months." I looked blankly at the sheet of paper in front of me.

"It could be less than that. We lost Sally yesterday. That's got people worried. If we lose any more leaders things will start to deteriorate fast."

There was a moment's bleak silence. "We need a game changer," I told Cody. He smiled slightly.

"I thought that's why we sent Jesse chasing off after his brother – to get some idea where people are taken when they're caught. Well, that, and because it got rid of him."

I ignored the jibe. "We need something else. Something that'll give us an edge."

The mocking smile became more pronounced. "And here it comes. The real reason you wanted to talk to me."

I ignored that as well. "We need to follow up on Glen's plan."

It took Cody a moment to figure out what I was talking about. "You mean setting up that GPS satellite locator he's always getting you and Noah to bring up at council meetings? That's what you want to pursue?"

"If we could contact people in the outside world, maybe even in America, we'd have a better idea what to do next. I mean, look around you..." I gestured at the paperwork covering every surface. "If we had more information about what things are like elsewhere, if we were able to ask questions, then we'd be better prepared for what could be coming."

He stood and thought for a long while, pacing back and forth. "Do you have a plan? One that would protect Glen?" he asked.

I smiled to myself. I had him. "Glen says the equipment is in Robert Gordon University, up in Garthdee. I thought that Blake, Glen and I could go along with one of Jeremy's supply runs. I know he's planning on heading up there soon to investigate the Asda. We could blend in and then sneak away to get it. There and back in a day, no problem."

"Sounds like you've got it all figured out. Shouldn't we have a council meeting about this?"

"Glen and Noah already agree, Jeremy will be glad of the help and Blake is always up for a dangerous mission. Including you and me we've got a majority. There'd only be Deborah left, and as long as she's looking after people she doesn't really care."

"What about Hazel?" he asked.

I cursed under my breath. I'd forgotten about her. "What about Hazel?" I asked him, one eyebrow raised.

He smiled that indecipherable smile again. "Fair enough. Then yes, you've got my support. Go for it as far as I'm concerned, but task Blake and his team with guarding Glen closely. Now, if you'll excuse me." He walked over to a table and picked up a box. I tilted my head, squinting to see the lid.

"A chess set?" I asked him.

"Percy's bored," he said nonchalantly. "I've been keeping him company and trying to amuse him."

"He plays chess?"

"I've been teaching him."

I looked at Cody oddly. He didn't usually go this far out of his way to be nice to people. More than that, there was something off about him, as if he'd been caught in a lie. I shook my head. Probably nothing.

I followed Cody out of the office and along the corridor. Just before we parted ways he turned to me, as if he'd forgotten something.

"I meant to ask. When will you be going on this mission?"

I smiled tightly at him. "Three days' time," I said. "Friday."

CHAPTER 11

It was six in the morning when I woke Blake up by knocking on his door, and he was not happy. I'd just finished hammering on wood for the third time when the door was wrenched open and he stuck his head out, hair still tousled from sleep.

"What is it?" he asked.

"Rise and shine," I said brightly. "We'll be setting off with Jeremy and the scavenging crew in about an hour."

"An hour?" Blake failed to stifle a yawn. "You said it would be tomorrow."

"Change of plan. Jeremy thought the sooner we get there and back the better."

That was a complete lie. Today was the day I'd told Jeremy we were leaving. He hadn't been happy about the early start either. But that was the whole point. We had to leave early in the morning before the others woke up so no one would see us.

It would take a while to move all the stuff from Asda back to the centre of town. The scavengers would be traipsing back and forth for several days. But Glen would only be going once and Jeremy was the only council member I'd told we were going today. If we were attacked, I would have proof that Jeremy was the traitor. After I eliminated him as a suspect, I could do the same again, finally working out who the spy was. But as the main aim of the mission was to get Glen's GPS satellite locator, we really didn't want to be attacked; Jeremy seemed the least likely traitor to me, so that's why I'd given him the correct information.

"I won't have time for breakfast," Blake muttered. "I hate fighting on an empty stomach."

I passed him the bowl of porridge I'd commandeered and his face lit up. "If we're lucky there won't be any fighting," I remarked.

He took the bowl and put it on a chest of drawers just inside the room. "Depends on your point of view. The more fighting the merrier for me!"

I tried not to roll my eyes. "Whatever. We're gathering in the foyer so get your group and meet us there. Oh, and Kyle wanted me to remind you to bring the empty bowl back."

We left just over an hour later. As I'd told Cody, Jeremy was taking his scavengers to check out an Asda up near Garthdee. He'd been reluctant to go before now because it was such a long way from the town centre. Blake and I were officially his extra protection. Glen was just another kid who'd volunteered to join the scavengers.

"Are you OK?" I asked Glen.

He nodded, slightly out of breath. Glen was one of the only people I knew who was still unfit in the chicken apocalypse.

"Never better. We're finally going to get the GPS satellite locator. I couldn't be happier."

"And you know that if we get into any trouble you're to run and hide, right? You don't need to prove yourself and fight."

He gave me a crooked smile. "You don't have to worry about that," he assured me.

He gamely chugged along, pushing one of the trolleys that would be used to transport our hoard back home.

Blake walked beside me, idly swinging his shock-stick. He looked perfectly happy. This was all an adventure to him.

"So how do you think this is going to go?" I asked.

He shrugged. "It's going to be a total mess. But with any luck I'll get a crack at the thing that got Sally."

I looked at him sidelong. "Do you really think it'll attack us? What would be the point?"

He returned my stare. "What would be the point? We've got two council members with us on this. Four if we count ourselves. We're the most tempting target around."

He was right: if the spy was going to report any target

to the chickens it would be us. I felt uncomfortable that Blake was saying it out loud.

"Not many people know that Glen's a council member, though. He doesn't get out much. Most people wouldn't even recognise him."

"True, I guess. Well, you never know. We could get lucky."

I turned to face him, annoyed. "This is serious."

He took a long look at me. "You've got to chill down, Your Ambassadorness. Fighting chickens is fun."

"Well, I don't think so."

He smirked and shook his head. "Nope, doesn't seem you do. Shame, you should try having fun sometimes. I thought someone who's such good friends with the famous Jesse would be up for more of a laugh."

I'd managed to not think about Jesse at all so far today. It had been a day and a half since we'd spoken on the radio, and I hadn't heard from him since. Hazel said if they got any information about him being captured she'd let me know, but I was still constantly worried.

"I'd laugh if Jesse ever said anything funny," I replied to Blake.

"You don't find him funny?"

"I find him tolerable. Just."

Blake just shook his head. "You're quackers."

A suspicion formed in my mind. "Are you copying Jesse, but with ducks instead of chickens?"

Blake went bright red and started walking faster.

"No. Why would I want to do that?"

I let him draw away. A wannabe Jesse. Who'd have thought it? The last thing we needed was more awful puns. Jesse had a lot to answer for.

It was almost midday when we decided to take a break. So far the walk had been mostly uphill. We'd actually passed very close to the chickens' old base in Beechgrove Terrace. There wasn't much left there now. The bomb I'd set off combined with the falling debris had pretty much flattened it. In the few weeks before the chickens came back Glen had poked around in there looking for useful stuff but he hadn't found anything. I know the Brotherhood had taken some things from there as well, though I didn't know what.

We sat by the side of the road and ate our sandwiches. They were all in little packets with our names on them. Kyle had probably made them specially. He usually did. He wasn't only good at organising rations, he was a fantastic chef. He even checked on people's allergies and preferences, hence the names on our sandwiches. I got corned beef and sweetcorn. It was oddly delicious.

All told it was mid-afternoon before we reached the Asda.

The plan was simple: while everyone else was busy rummaging through stock, Blake, Glen and I would split off and go to the university campus, which was right up the hill. We should make it back in time to help load up trolleys and push them back. Even if we were missed it wasn't that unusual for people to wander off. We could just say we'd gone to the B&Q across the road and no one would bat an eyelid.

The interior of the Asda was dark. We crowded around the entrance, like thieves before a cave. Jeremy stood and turned, addressing us.

"OK, guys, you know the drill. Once we're inside it's going to be dark so everyone put on your head torches. We need tins, chocolate and batteries. They're the most important things. After that get bottled drinks, anything that looks interesting. I want as much stuff as you can grab in the next hour then we're heading back."

He looked at me, Blake and Glen and pointed towards the B&Q.

"There's another store over there," he told us cheerfully. "I'll send you guys to check it out later, if you don't mind."

We didn't need the huge wink he gave us, but I felt grateful nonetheless. He was giving us a good backstory for when we had to slip away.

Once inside the Asda, we switched on our torches. The playpen to the side of the entrance was spooky, abandoned when it should have been full of kids. I'd been in there a few times myself. It was a fun place to spend an afternoon while Mum did the grocery shopping. Blake turned to one of his guys.

"Stay by the door," he muttered. "Make sure nothing comes in or out."

"What's that smell?" Glen asked, wrinkling his nose. I could smell it too, mould and rotten things, like a gym bag that had been lying forgotten in a cupboard all summer.

"That's the fruit, vegetables, milk, bread. Just about anything that can decay really," Jeremy replied cheerfully. He handed us a mouth protector each. "Wear these, it helps. When all this is over someone's going to have an awful time cleaning up this mess and it's not going to be me."

We found the tins and Jeremy walked about with a clipboard, making notes of what was there, what we were taking and what had to be left behind. There was a good haul in this place. There can't have been many kids living around here and the stores had hardly been touched. A happy clinking filled the air as tins were piled into trolleys and people began cracking jokes. Everything was going really well and I was just thinking about heading up to the university...

When we heard the scream.

We all fell silent. The darkness suddenly seemed a lot more oppressive than it had a moment ago, and the torchlight no longer looked jolly, just dim and creepy. Someone broke the silence with a nervous chuckle.

"OK, who's having a laugh? No mucking around, OK?"

No one answered.

"Is everyone here?" I asked.

There was a quick counting of heads – not easy with

each others' torches shining in our eyes – and we found someone was missing.

"Alright, split up," ordered Jeremy. "Find Stevey. And if he's having a laugh I'll kill him."

"No, we can't do that," Glen exclaimed.

Everyone turned to him. "Why not?" asked Jeremy slightly agressively.

"Haven't you ever seen *Scooby Doo*? Something bad always happens when they split up."

That helped to lighten the atmosphere a bit. I felt myself momentarily missing Jesse and his jokes. He'd probably have said something similar.

"Well, don't be Shaggy then," Jeremy said and everyone split into small groups.

Glen stuck close to Blake and me. I had half a mind to suggest we leave then. No one would notice us go. But they might waste time looking for us. And if there really was something in here, and it wasn't just Stevey having a laugh or wandering off, I didn't want to abandon them.

Blake led us back to the main door, where his guard was standing nervously, looking back into the store.

"Have you seen anything?" Blake asked.

The guy shook his head. "It was all quiet until the scream," he said. "What's going on?"

Blake shrugged. "I don't know. Stay here and call if you see anything. Be on your guard; there's something about this I don't like."

"You and me both, Blake," the boy said but he stayed where he was, standing guard faithfully.

We trekked back into the darkness and headed towards the cluster of bobbing head torches.

"Have you found Stevey?" I asked the others.

"Yep," came back Jeremy's grim voice. "Come and see."

I hurried over and looked down at a shape lying on the floor. It was Stevey and he was unconscious. And not just any kind of unconsciousness. I recognised it.

"Oh no," I muttered to Blake. "It's here."

He nodded back, something of a smile on his face. "The chicken from yesterday. I get to fight it."

I was more interested in what this meant. Only Jeremy had known we were coming on this trip today. Was he the spy?

Glen seemed to be paying more attention to the scavengers. They were shifting around, looking uneasy. "I think we should get out of here," one of them muttered.

Jeremy stared at Stevey's unconscious body for a second then nodded. "Grab his arms someone. We'd better get where we can actually see what's going on."

We pulled Stevey along the slick tile floor as gently as we could. Just as we were reaching the door something occurred to me. "Do we have everyone?" I asked.

Another quick headcount revealed that we were two short.

This time the screams were blood-curdling.

Something broke inside the scavengers. They dropped Stevey's arms and ran for the door. Jeremy ran after them fast, getting ahead and throwing out his arms.

"Now, wait a moment. There are more of us than there is of it. We're not going to abandon Stevey just because we're spooked. Now get back there and grab him."

And that's when the darkness came alive and ate him.

It was like Sally all over again. Plating seemed to materialise from mid-air and crawl over Jeremy's skin, enveloping him. Jeremy barely had time for a startled expression before being yanked backwards and away. And replacing him was the black mask of a chicken's face.

The next ten minutes were a muddle of confusion. We all panicked and scattered, the head torches' dancing beams adding to the craziness of the situation. The robot chicken strode between us, striking out with its wings and buffeting us over. It seemed to be everywhere. Blake would charge towards it, swinging his shock-stick and half blinding everyone, and it would melt away only to reappear again behind us.

Blake bellowed at us, herding us into place. Slowly, he regained some sense of order.

"People with shock-sticks, form a circle. Everyone else get inside it. If that thing comes at us again, it will live to regret it."

Minutes passed slowly and nothing happened. Blake was beside me in the circle.

"D'you think it's gone?" I muttered to him out of the corner of my mouth.

He shook his head, his voice tight with anger. "I hope not. I need another crack at it."

"Look," someone said in a hushed whisper and pointed towards the door. A shadow appeared there, the silhouette of a huge chicken. It turned its head, looking here and there, eyes gleaming a pale green in the darkness. We huddled closer together, getting ready for its attack. Eventually it strutted outside and away.

It was a while before we felt convinced that it was really gone. We spent the next half hour searching the store for people who'd been knocked out or forced to hide. But as the afternoon wore on we had to accept the truth.

We'd lost another council member.

And all that was left behind was a shiny black feather.

CHAPTER 12

After the darkness inside, the weak sun was blinding as we left the Asda. The scavengers didn't speak much, just collected the trolleys that we'd already filled and set off home. They just wanted to get far away as fast as possible.

I was ready to go with them. But Glen wouldn't let me.

"We're so close," he said to me and Blake in a stage whisper as we held a small meeting. "We just have to walk up that hill and we're there."

"He's right," Blake said shortly. He wasn't very happy about being shown up by the chicken.

"I don't know," I said, chewing my bottom lip. "It feels like a big risk. We should get home while we have the chance."

"Please, Rayna," Glen said, tugging on my sleeve. "We won't get another chance. There's no way the council will let me try again after this. Everyone will vote against it."

"It would be a waste not to try," Blake agreed.

"We've already been attacked once. I don't think it'll happen again. We were sent here for a reason so we should finish the job."

"Alright but we've got to be quick." I didn't have much choice but to agree.

The university campus wasn't far away. We trudged up the hill, Glen, Blake and what was left of his crew. Some of them had been taken out by the chicken and were snoring away in the trolleys being pushed home, along with Stevey. Those of us who were left didn't talk much. I don't know about the others but I had my own reasons for keeping silent.

I was scared.

More than scared, I was terrified. Completely and utterly petrified.

It felt uncomfortable. I hadn't been this scared of the chickens since the night I'd seen my sister get taken. Sure, I'd never been happy to see them, and when I was close to getting caught once or twice I'd been scared. But not this way. This was different. This chicken was so much more terrifying than the others. I didn't want to ever face that thing again, see that blank expression so close to my face, those weird green eyes. I was frightened. Plain and simple.

But more than that, I was annoyed. If we were attacked today then Jeremy should have been the spy. That was the whole point of my plan. Perhaps it wasn't such a great plan after all. Now that Jeremy had been taken we were back at square one and down a council member. Just one step closer to that line on Cody's chart.

The Robert Gordon University campus came into view at the crest of the hill, just round a bend. Now we faced the slight problem of figuring out how to reach it. We tried going down an obvious path that led to the walkway below, but iron handrails blocked our way. In the end we just clambered over them and tramped across the grass and some roses that were beginning to wilt. Autumn was almost here. It was nearly a year since the chickens had first attacked. Scary.

There was no electricity, but it was easy enough just to prise open the automatic doors. Then we were in.

In contrast to the Aberdeen University glass-cube library where Glen had spent the first part of the war, someone had gone to a lot of trouble to make this place look nice. The modern space had an intelligent futuristic feel. There was a wide white wall at the far end of a curving high corridor. This must be the atrium. There were several walkways for people to bustle along and look important and a few bridges over a long corridor. Off to the right there was an area shaped like some sort of gladiatorial pit. Maybe a reading area? The lights in there were made to look like pine cones.

Glen was looking around with wide eyes, obviously loving everything he was seeing. He spotted a sign for the Computing Department, grabbed my arm and pulled me along. "Come on, this way," he cried, practically dragging me. I dug in my heels, slowing him down.

"Careful, Doc," I said, using Jesse's nickname for him. "Don't run too far ahead. Keep together and move slowly. That way we can protect you, as well as each other and not get ambushed."

"Alright. Though I don't think that thing's going to be back. Is it?" He looked at me sideways, suddenly unsure.

I didn't know what to say. On the one hand I wanted to reassure him. On the other I couldn't promise the giant black chicken wouldn't be back. But Blake interrupted anyway.

"I hope it does," he said, swinging him shock-stick menacingly. "This time we'll get to deal with it properly. No hiding in the dark. Just a fair five-on-one fight."

Blake's crew all nodded confidently at his words. I looked at Glen and shrugged. "What he said," I told him.

Glen seemed to accept that and started off again. I followed, keeping an eye on my surroundings. I didn't think it would show up again. But it never hurt to be careful.

Glen led us up some stairs to a computer lab. Then he started rummaging about. I watched, alarmed. "Hey, Glen," I said. "How long do you think this is going to take?"

"I'll let you know when I've found it," he told me. I didn't like the sound of that. I had assumed that he'd somehow know where it would be. There was nothing to do but wait and be vigilant.

Until one of Blake's guys who'd been standing sentry came running up. "Bad news, guys," he said. "It's back."

He pointed out the window and I followed the direction of his finger.

There it was, stalking across the grass, the same as we'd done, its beak to the ground as if following our scent. For the first time I got a good view of it. It looked like a chicken, obviously, but more sleek. Its feathers seemed individually cut and rustled slightly as it moved. Except on the wings, which looked like solid slabs of steel. Green orbs glowed in place of eyes – the only colour on it, everything else was menacing black. It looked up at our building a few times and I had to tell myself that it couldn't see us.

Blake cursed softly and joyously under his breath. "Found what you're looking for yet?" he asked.

"No... not yet," Glen replied, anxious. "I need more time."

"Then I guess it's our job to buy you that time." Blake jerked his head from side to side, cracking his neck. Then he cracked his knuckles. Carefully he took off his heavy jacket and laid it on the ground. The others did the same.

"Come on, team. Let's see how *it* likes being ambushed for once. Rayna, you stay here and look after Glen. And start composing some epic victory songs."

He ran off, his crew snapping at his heels. Crazy. They were absolutely crazy.

Glen kept searching, but I turned back to the window. I wanted to see what would happen next.

The chicken stalked up to the same door we'd come through. Blake and his team had vanished. The huge black robot walked through the door and looked right up at me. It took a menacing step forward.

"Get it lads!"

The chicken hunters swarmed up from behind the reception desk and charged at the giant bird. It hopped back, its wings spread, as if trying to flutter away.

"Hailey, entangle it. Get it into the pit thing!"

One of the group pulled a chain from some pocket deep in her jacket and whipped it at the chicken's leg, tugging sharply. The rest poked at it with their sticks. They drove it back to the lip of the sunken pit I'd noticed earlier then forced it in.

Blake stroke forward. "Not so tough now, are you?" he taunted and swung his shock-stick.

I thought I saw the chicken's eyes flash. It raised a wing and the staff bounced off it with no effect. It looked angry.

Blake stepped back and settled down into a boxing stance. "This just got interesting."

I returned to Glen, who was kneeling next to some boxes, playing with some sticky notes. "We've got a little bit of time."

"Good," he said, getting to his feet. "Let's get going."

For the next ten minutes Glen and I searched room after room, Glen scribbling in his notebook as he went. Although the university looked pretty, I wish it had been better organised. If I ever get to design a university it will have lots of arrows all over the place saying things like, 'Emergency transmitters this way!'

Finally our luck ran out. As we hurried along the next walkway we witnessed the chicken and Blake's crew in a battle of the ages.

I'll say it again, as I've said it before. They might be crazy. They might be downright insane. But Blake and his crew certainly knew how to fight. Four of them stood with their shock-sticks glowing in their hands against the dark mass that was the chicken. One already lay on the ground, stick lying a few inches from her fingertips.

The rest of the crew were putting up a good fight. They danced around the robot, hitting it several times all over its body, changing direction, jumping over strikes and generally making a nuisance of themselves. Blake was right in among them, always trying to strike the chicken's face and hold its attention while his crew did what they did best. The robot struck at them with its wings but they either dodged or blocked with their sticks, throwing up glowing blue sparks. I couldn't believe they'd held it off for ten minutes.

But as valiant as they were, it was all in vain. At the end of the day they couldn't hurt the chicken, and it only had to land a glancing blow for the shock in its wings to incapacitate them. Someone was swept out of the air with a lucky flick, someone else wasn't quite fast enough to jump a hefty clawed kick. One by one they fell, until only Blake was left.

He gave a scream of rage and charged forward, swinging his shock-stick hard. The chicken turned sharply, just brushing Blake with the edge of its wing, but that was enough. The sparks flew and Blake was felled at last.

Then the chicken turned and stared directly at us.

"Oh no," I moaned and grabbed Glen's hand, pulling him along. He hadn't been following the fight; he'd been scribbling frantically in his notebook the whole time. Maybe he was making up the epic song Blake had requested. Though I was scathing of the guy, I had to admit he kind of deserved it after that performance.

We ran through corridors, then stopped when we realised our boots were making a lot of noise against the pristine white floor. I glanced wildly around, Glen waiting for my instructions.

"Get in here and stay quiet." I pulled him into a room and we hid behind a desk. Through the glass panel of the door we watched the corridor outside.

Then we heard it: a gentle *tap-tap-tapping* that echoed strangely around us. I felt the goosebumps shiver and migrate across my skin.

It was coming.

Closer and closer the sound came: *tap, tap, tap, tap.*

A shadow passed across the door and I stared at it in mute horror, praying that it would pass.

It slowed and stopped, looked around with those awful green eyes. I felt the sudden mad impulse to laugh, to jump out and scare it. But I knew it was just the fear talking. I bit down on it, suppressing the urge. I mustn't lose it. I had to keep control. For Glen if no one else.

I looked around to see how he was dealing with the situation. He was still scribbling in that notebook. I stared at him, bemused. What on earth was he doing?

Then the tapping came again. I looked back round and saw the shadow move off. The chicken must have decided we were deeper inside the building. That worked fine for me.

"Look," I whispered to Glen, "we can't outrun it but it can't stay here forever. If we don't report back, Noah will probably come get us armed with lasers. We just need to hide and wait it out."

"Uh-huh?" he said, not really looking at me.

I frowned at him. "What are you doing?" I asked.

"Nothing." He tore the paper out of his notebook and scrunched it into a ball. "Should we go back and get the satellite GPS? I think I know which components to take now."

"Yeah. Now, while the coast is clear. Then hide."

I straightened up and moved towards the door. I listened momentarily, pressing my ear up against the glass, keeping beneath the level of the window.

I couldn't hear anything.

"I think it's safe," I said. I grasped the door handle and pulled it open.

The chicken peered down at us from its perch on a high beam, its comb raised and proud. It looked at us expressionlessly for a moment and I felt my mouth gape open. It had known where we were the entire time and was just playing with us.

"Get back!" I jumped backwards, trying to swing the door closed. But it flew down and cannoned into the door before it was completely shut. I dug in my heels, forcing all my weight into resisting but it was no good. The chicken was too strong. The soles of my shoes made sad squeaking noises as they were slowly forced back. Then all at once the door gave way and the chicken was in.

I stumbled backwards and it ignored me, heading straight for Glen. With no time to draw my shock-stick I just threw myself after it, catching it on the shoulder and wrapping my arms around its neck.

"Get. Away. From. Him," I said through gritted teeth. "Glen, run!"

It rocked slightly, swaying beneath my weight and motion, then swung around. I'd seen videos of people riding the rodeo on YouTube and it felt just like that. It bucked and shook, trying everything to loosen my grip. Eventually it just started to spin, round and round and round and round. My hands began to loosen and then I was flung off, crashing into a desk.

Glen had been standing very still while all this was happening. Maybe he believed that old story about chickens not being able to see things that weren't in motion. Maybe that was generally true, but it wasn't in this situation. The chicken definitely knew where Glen was and it advanced, mockingly.

At the last moment Glen dodged to the side and ran towards me. The chicken pecked at him but missed.

I got to my feet, groaning, as the chicken completed its turn and darted forward. Glen was there, hands out as if trying to pull me towards him.

I saw the whole awful thing as if in slow motion. I felt Glen's hand connect with mine and grasp it. Behind his shoulder I could see the chicken looming close. Its whole chest area swung open like a giant mouth, reaching forward to swallow Glen whole. Then it was closing around him, little talons seeming to reach from inside and pull him away from me. I held on to his arm for as long as I could but I felt his fingers slip from mine. At the last moment I looked up into his face and saw that he wasn't scared. His face showed something worse than fear: acceptance.

"Say hello to America for me," he said. Then the chicken pulled him backwards and enveloped him.

It shook once or twice, as if making sure that Glen was secure. Then it just turned and strutted towards the door. It didn't even run, like it didn't consider me a threat. I sprinted forward, screaming wordlessly, then had to dodge a swiftly struck wing. I spun clumsily, slipping and falling, hitting my head on the floor. An awful iron pain crashed through my skull and I saw stars. By the time I was able to crawl back to my feet the chicken was long gone.

I slumped down heavily.

Glen had been taken.

Three councillors captured from right under my nose. And it was three too many.

Something finally managed to pierce the hazy fog in my head, and I looked down at my hand. It was still clenched in a fist, not having opened since Glen's hold had been wrenched away. I uncurled my fingers and stared down, confused...

At the scrunched-up ball of paper Glen had slipped there just before he was taken.

CHAPTER 13

It was pretty late by the time we got home. The street lamps had come on, glowing a dull orange, making everything seem gloomy and washed out. The trolley we'd taken with us rattled along, a wheel squeaking every so often and getting on our nerves.

I was glad we had it though. Otherwise we wouldn't have been able to transport the five black boxes that housed the GPS satellite locator and all its components. The note Glen had slipped me told me which ones to take and how to set it up. He must have thought the chicken would have destroyed the devices if it had caught us with them. I wish Glen had decided to run instead.

I brightened up slightly when we reached the hotel. Because there, waiting for us, looking battered but very much alive, was Percy. I might not get on with him all that well, but it had been unsettling not having him around.

"The council's waiting for you," he told us as we trooped up. "They heard about what happened with Jeremy."

I nodded wearily and plodded wearily into the building. Blake followed after, directing the rest of his crew towards the hospital. Percy trudged along behind us. None of us spoke.

The council was in mid discussion when we walked in. Noah turned and smiled at me, half rising to greet us. Then his eyes flitted from one of us to another and he noted the lack of Glen. His eyes showed his sadness and he sat back down.

"Rayna, Blake. Care to tell us what happened?"

That was Cody, getting straight to business as usual. Percy walked up and stood behind him, a towering shadow, silently backing him up.

I looked at Blake and decided to answer. "We went to get the satellite GPS that Glen wanted. As you know we'd decided to blend in with one of Jeremy's scouting groups to be a less obvious target. We were ambushed twice by this... new type of chicken. The first time it managed to get Jeremy. The second time Glen sacrificed himself so that we could get the GPS satellite locator."

Hazel looked at me and frowned. "Wait, you were going to get that today? I thought you were doing that on Saturday."

"I thought it was Sunday," Deborah added. "You asked me to have medical supplies ready, just in case everything went wrong."

Cody's face didn't move, though I sensed a wave of anger drifting off him. "Yes and I was told Friday. Care to say why you were lying to us all?"

I looked at Noah desperately. He nodded quickly. "It's because we needed to test you," he said.

Cody's eyes narrowed. "Test us? How?"

"Someone here is a spy."

I'd expected there to be a commotion at those words but everyone was deathly silent. I swallowed then continued. "The chickens know what we're doing far too well for it to be a coincidence. Someone here is feeding them information. I thought if I gave each of you different information we'd uncover the spy."

"And?" Cody urged.

I shrugged helplessly. "Jeremy was the only one who knew we were setting out today and he was the first one captured. Unless he was interrogated or something..."

"But there wasn't time for that." Blake looked at me angrily. I guess he wasn't happy that I thought he might be a spy.

"Look, it's obvious who the spy is." Blake pointed at Hazel. "It's them. They fit in with the rest of us like a duck out of water."

Hazel glared at him. "What exactly do we have to do to convince you that we're on your side?"

"What do you know about this new chicken?" Noah quickly cut in, trying to keep the peace.

Cody was watching us all with glittering eyes, Percy glowering at his shoulder. Deborah seemed annoyed but no more than usual. I looked sideways to see Blake glaring at Hazel and Hazel glaring back. Which one could be the spy?

Hazel looked away and pulled her backpack up onto the table. "We've been looking into this new chicken. And we came up with this."

She pulled a roll of paper from her bag and spread it out on the table. It was a copy of the blueprints of the chicken we'd fought against. A title at the top said we were fighting the C-800 model.

I looked at it, frowning. Where did she get that from?

I wasn't the only one. "Who gave you those?" Cody asked.

Hazel shrugged. "We found the blueprints in one of the warehouse cupboards. I guess they must have been designing it there." She quickly moved on. "From what we can see, this is a single-target creature. It's got enough room to store one person. The chest opens up and the human is stored there. As soon as the chest is closed a gas is emitted, putting the prisoner to sleep."

"So that means it's definitely targeting the council," Noah said. "They're not just scooping up random kids."

Hazel looked at him and nodded. "That's right," she said.

"How do we beat it?" Blake asked. Hazel turned back to the blueprints.

"It's not going to be easy," she told him. "The hull is bullet-proof, and resistant to electricity. The wings can be charged, shocking anyone they hit."

Blake rubbed his arm. "Yeah, we got that," he said.

Hazel looked at him and nodded absently. "Honestly? Against this, your best chance is to run."

"Run?" Blake shook his head. "Not an option."

Hazel sighed. "Use your head. The suit is super-fast and super-strong but that comes at a price. The battery isn't very big and it won't be able to work for long periods of time. It's got a very simple goal: get in, get the target, get out. The further you can get the target from this thing the better your chances are that the battery will run down and it'll have to turn back."

"What are we calling it?" Cody asked idly.

"The Chickenator." Everyone turned to look at me. I shrugged. "That's what Jesse would call it."

Cody sighed, though a few people round the table had smiles on their faces. "Even when he's not here he's causing mischief. Fine, Chickenator works. Now, is outrunning it the only thing we can do? Can't we cut off its connection to the signal?"

Hazel shook her head. "No, it's got some sort of replicator deep inside its head, very well protected. Basically it mimics the signal so it can never be cut off. Pretty nifty really."

I didn't like to hear the admiration in her voice, but Blake spoke before I could say anything. "So there's no way for us to fight that thing?"

"Hit it enough times and it might feel something. The wings are the most shielded but aim for the body and you could do some damage. And of course there's no shielding inside, so hitting it while it's chest is open should work. But I'd try running first. This thing is near impossible to beat."

Blake smiled slightly. "I don't run."

Hazel rolled her eyes. "Well, good luck with that. The Brotherhood will try and make something to help, but it'll take days. Let's just hope that it's done for now."

"This is a serious piece of hardware," Cody said from the top of the table. "Why is it coming after us?"

"You haven't worked it out yet?" We all looked at Noah. He scowled back, confused. "But it's obvious."

There was silence for a moment. "Apparently not," Cody said. "What's obvious?"

"We're a testing ground."

"He's right," Hazel said. "We are. I mean, up until now I think we were just a training ground for Catchers before they were sent out to fight national armies. But it looks as if they're taking us more seriously."

Cody pulled out a notebook and started scribbling away. "A testing ground? So everything they throw at us will eventually be used against other countries? The Chickenator," he sighed, "could be used to kidnap the President of the USA or something?"

"Maybe," Noah said. "I mean that would make sense."

"I'm going to have to think about this." Cody closed his notebook and stood up. "Is that all?"

Noah looked at him aghast. "We've just lost another

two council members. We haven't even replaced Sally yet. We need to talk about that."

"Then hold votes or something. If anyone wants to make a target of themselves then good for them." He started walking towards the door.

"Cody, stop." Noah got up and grabbed his arm as he passed. Percy took a step forward but Cody waved him back.

"We've lost three people. We don't just need to fill their positions. We need to take a moment and think about them. About them being gone. Don't you care about that?"

"It's not my job to care." Cody shook himself loose and began stalking away again. "It's my job to find us a way out of this. That's all."

He was almost out of the room when Noah shouted one last thing after him, "I know you care for some people, Cody. I *know* it."

Cody paused slightly. Then the door closed and he was gone.

After Cody left, the rest of us sat around and talked about the ones who weren't there. Even Percy stayed for a while, though he mostly just sat and listened. I guess he was doing it to report back to Cody later but it felt nice having him there. Noah offered to take over as Head of Communications but we couldn't come to any other solid plans. Eventually we decided to get some sleep and look for volunteers in the morning.

I lay in my bed and thought about the day. What a complete disaster. I hadn't found the spy. Jeremy and Glen had been taken. The only good thing was that we'd got the communications equipment, though I had no idea what we'd actually do with it.

And to top it all off, I'd had to tell the council there was a spy among them. So whoever it was, they knew I was on to them. Not only that but it put up walls between council members, stopped them from trusting each other. I'd even seen some of them give me funny looks as they were leaving.

I felt a sudden stab of sympathy for Hazel and rolled over, staring at the wall. She hadn't spoken to me as she'd left, taking the Chickenator blueprints with her. She hadn't even looked at me. I'd have to apologise to her in the morning.

Although... where had she found those blueprints? Had the chickens really been working on the Chickenator for so long that they'd left them behind in the warehouse when we drove them out? Or did the Brotherhood still have some connection with the chickens? More than ever I wanted to know where she was getting her information.

I frowned. There was something bothering me. Something that wasn't about the disastrous day or Hazel's weirdly accurate knowledge. Something that was missing.

Jesse hadn't contacted me.

He'd promised he would call at exactly nine tonight. He wanted to know if my plan had worked. But it was almost ten and I hadn't heard anything from him. The walkie-talkie rested on my bedside table where I always left it, plugged into the wall, the red light staring at me through the darkness. Hazel had even hooked up a recorder to it so Jesse could leave messages but when I checked there was nothing.

I fidgeted for a moment then picked up the walkie-talkie. Jesse had talked about heading back soon. He wouldn't be sneaking about tonight.

I pressed the button. "Jesse?" I said into the speaker. "Jesse, are you there?"

No reply.

"Jesse? Jesse, I really need to talk."

Just static.

I kept trying, more and more frantically, for over an hour. Then I finally gave up.

Whatever had happened, Jesse was no longer answering.

CHAPTER 14

JESSE: Operation Henhouse Hustle

If you've ever wondered what the inside of a Catcher looks like, I can tell you: nothing special. I'd had nightmares about being pecked up and captured. Honestly, it was like going down a slide and landing in a small round metal room. I lay on my back, throwing a ball at the wall as the world lurched around me. The Catcher was heading back to the barn.

What came next wasn't so pleasant.

A hatch in the floor opened up and a Commando stuck its head through. I caught the ball as it bounced back at me and waved cheerily.

"Take me to your leader," I said.

The chicken just stared at me for a second then bobbed out of sight. The hatch was left open but I stayed where I was. It was comfy.

Then the floor lurched, throwing me out.

I landed hard on the dusty floor of a room in the huge barn and groaned. Taking my time, I eased myself to my feet and looked around.

This seemed to be where the Catchers were loaded and unloaded. There was a ton of them, standing about empty.

It was pretty creepy. The place bustled though. Chickens were everywhere, swarming over different machines. I saw a couple that looked like bulkier versions of Commandos, which could weld things with lasers from their eyes. I guess they were egg-ineers.

Coloured lines were painted on the floor. A Commando fixed its beady eye on me and jerked its head meaningfully at one of them. I guess I had to follow the line. It led across the loading area, through a door into a dimly lit space beyond.

I walked carefully down the path the Commando had indicated to me. One walked in front of me and one behind, making sure I didn't step out of line. It was very tempting to just kick one of them, but I know I wouldn't get anything out of it except a stubbed toe and a clawed leg. I had to bide my time.

That didn't mean I couldn't have some fun.

I glanced around, trying to see something I could make a pun out of. To the left and right were rows of cages, wire mesh stretched tight across wooden frames. Shapes lurked in the dim glow, human silhouettes that looked up at me briefly before going back to whatever they were doing. The Commando in front of me carefully steered me towards the right and I could see that hundreds of cages stretched off all around us.

"I must say I'm impressed," I said cheerfully. My escorts didn't make any indication that they'd heard, so I continued, "I thought you were supposed to keep the fox out of the henhouse but here you are. You got all the foxes you could find and stuck them in here."

I thought I heard a soft chuckle off to my right but it was lost in the smothering gloom. The Commandos ignored me.

Finally we came to a cage with just one occupant sitting away from the door. The Commandos eyed it suspiciously then one flapped a wing. The door swung open.

The figure inside lunged at them. In one smooth motion the Commandos pushed me into the cage, sending us both sprawling, then slammed the door behind me.

"Jesse? Is that you?"

I painfully untangled myself from the person already in the cage and sat up. She just lay there, astonished, her long blonde hair hanging half over her face.

"Hi Sally."

The ex-council-member stared at me for a moment, open-mouthed. "What are you doing here?" she asked.

"Same thing as you, I guess. I got caught."

"I thought you'd been caught a week ago! We went so long without hearing from you."

I winced. "Yes, Rayna mentioned that. At length. But I'm fine. What happened to you?"

"Oh, it was awful. One moment we were scaring off Catchers that were attacking the farm, the next something jumped out of a bush at me. I got snatched, then I felt all woozy and passed out. I woke up here!"

"That sounds like a bad eggs-perience. Do you know what took you?"

"Nope. I just know the chickens call it 'The Indonesian'. I think its name might be Cemani. Jesse, this chicken is serious business. It hates humans."

"They all hate humans."

"Not in the same way as this one. It despises us. It'll do everything in its power to hurt and belittle us."

That sounded terrible. "When I get out I'll warn Rayna and the others. They'll be prepared for whatever it can do to them."

"You're getting out?"

I winked at her. "Of course I am. This is all part of my master plan."

"Your master plan?"

"That's right."

"Which involved you getting caught?"

"Yes."

She looked at me. "It's working so far then. What exactly is your plan?"

"Well," I looked around cautiously, worried about being heard, "I thought I'd give myself up for capture and see what the inside of this place is like. Check out the defences and stuff, you know?"

She nodded determinedly. "Of course. What'll you do next?"

"I'm planning on being a double agent. I'll pretend to go over and work for the chickens but in reality I'll be undermining them from the inside. Good, eh?"

Sally stared at me then blinked slowly. "Jesse... that's a terrible idea."

"I've asked to see their leader, but who knows if they listened. I'll keep ruffling their feathers until they take me to him."

Sally reached out and grabbed my arm firmly. "And you can't tell him anything. He'll just pump you for information and then send you straight back to the prison cells. You'll just give away information for no reason."

"How do you know that?"

"There was someone else who had the same idea. He got picked up just like you from outside barn and asked to see the leader. King Cluck just laughed at him, and made an example of him. Told us not to even attempt to outwit our chicken masters."

"This guy, what's his name?"

"Ethan."

"My brother's called Ethan! Where is he? Can I see him? What's...?"

Sally crawled to my side and slapped a hand over my mouth. "Not so loud," she whispered sharply. "They're listening. And if they know you've got a brother here they might use you against each other."

I prized Sally's hand away from my mouth. It tasted like dirt. "Do they do that?"

"Yes! Of course they do that. Threatening family members is like their favourite thing to do."

I nodded and lowered my voice to a whisper. "Alright. But do you know where he is?"

"Nope. As punishment for his disobedience, they trussed him up 'like a chicken' and wheeled him round in a giant roasting tin for us all to see. He was yelling a lot so they shoved an apple in his mouth and tied a paper beak over it. When the ropes were finally cut, he got kind of mad and tried to pick on a Catcher."

"How'd that go?"

"He's still in their top-security cell, so not that well."

Poor Ethan; he'd been captured after all. Suddenly I felt very stupid. I'd massively under-egg-stimated our chicken foe. "So I gave myself up for nothing? I'm just stuck here now?"

"That depends." She was still crouched very close to me, speaking softly but with an intense edge to her voice. I could suddenly see why she'd been picked for the council; Sally was a tough old bird under that soft exterior. "If you got out would you come back for the rest of us?"

"Of course," I said. "That was the whole point of my plan."

"Then, if you get to see King Cluck, we'll cause a diversion while you're in the control room. It should draw most of them away. It'll be your best chance."

"We?" Then I looked around and saw that the whispered conversation I'd been having with Sally wasn't so private. The people in the cages around us were leaning in, listening intently. Someone gave me a thumbs-up when he saw me, another saluted mockingly. "You think it would work?"

"You can't let them win, Jesse. And you've got to warn the council about the thing that took me."

There was a *tap-tap-tapping* in the distance of claws getting closer.

Everyone in the cages around me shuffled about, pretending they hadn't just been listening in. Sally grabbed me in a quick, fierce hug.

"Green lever in the control room," she whispered into

my ear. "There's a bunch of lasers attached to the outside of this building. The buttons beside it select all of the targets. Push it up to fire at the targets. Pull it down to shoot everything else. Give us twenty minutes."

"Tell my brother hello from me," I whispered back.

She pulled away and grinned. "You got it."

Behind me the door to the cage swung open.

"Time to go," the Commando intoned. "Our Leader will talk to you now."

CHAPTER 15

RAYNA: Aberdeen

My dad always said I tended to overreact. Whenever something happened to me I would hit back harder. He said he was proud of me for being so passionate about stuff. Of course he probably never expected me to break into my sister's warehouse in the middle of the night just because I'd not heard from my best friend for a few days.

The guards went past for the third time. It was easy enough to hear them. They marched to a rhythm, chanting to stay in time. It sounded like they were going, "Bawk, bawk, bawk," to the same tune as the guards from *The Wizard of Oz*. I stayed crouched in the shadows, counting under my breath. I was wearing loose, dark clothes, which allowed me to creep around unseen. Logically I knew the Brotherhood wouldn't have hurt Jesse. They loved him, hung on his every word. Half the reason they'd given us the walkie-talkies was because they wanted to know as much as I did that he was safe.

But there's a difference between knowing something and feeling it. While part of my mind calmly told me the facts, the passionate bit was screaming that the Brotherhood had kept secrets from me before. They had some way of gathering information that they weren't telling anyone about. I had to find out what it was. And maybe even use it to find out what had happened to Jesse.

The next pair of guards went past and this time I followed them, keeping low to the ground, trainers landing without a sound. I watched them carefully, avoiding the light thrown by their shock-sticks.

The first obstacle I had to pass was a low wall, built out of bricks by the Brotherhood, which stretched all around the warehouse. It barely came up to my waist but it was high enough to deter Commandos. The guards patrolled the inside of the wall, keeping their eyes out for silhouettes of chickens trying to fly over. They worked in pairs, with eight people circling the building at any one time.

There was a slight weakness though: a brief moment when one group had turned a corner, leaving a blind spot before the next pair approached.

I crouched down behind the wall in the blind spot, letting the pair ahead of me walk on, still counting under my breath. I saw them turn the corner and knew another couple would come past soon. Still as a mouse I waited, almost holding my breath. I heard the "Bawk, bawk, bawk" chanting get louder and someone rubbing their hands. There was the *thud, thud, thud* of footsteps and then they were right beside me. I froze, thinking for a moment how stupid I was to be hiding here. They just needed to look over the wall. There was no way I wouldn't be seen.

Then they were past me, their voices beginning to fade. I waited a moment then flipped over the wall and began stalking after them, trying to keep myself as low as possible.

We rounded the corner and there was no yell behind me. It seemed that I'd got away with it. So far so good.

I kept to the shadows and followed the watch around the building a good four times before I worked out what to do next. The warehouse was in good repair, with no holes to sneak through. I guess it was chicken proof. There was a large sliding door that would be used to drag Catchers in and out. Beside it was a normal, human-sized door, with a handle high on the side, inaccessible to chickens' claws. I would have to go in that way. And I'd have to do it soon. Dawn was coming.

I waited until the pair I was following had gone just past the door then darted towards it, praying it wasn't locked. I got lucky; it opened easily. I slipped inside before the next pair rounded the corner.

The inside of the warehouse was creepy, weird shapes looming out of the darkness towards me. I shrank away from a half-dismantled Catcher that rose from the gloom like a dinosaur. I shook myself out of it and crept on.

It was at this point that I realised I had no idea what I was searching for.

Still it was interesting looking around. I got out my head torch, hoping that if they spotted me they'd just assume I was a member of the Brotherhood. Even the little light made things better. I could see they were busy making more lasers from dismantled Catcher heads. In a corner, tucked away to the side, was a small table with half-built shock-sticks laid out. Beside it stood an empty Commando suit.

I stopped, and a paralysing sense of horror flooded down my spine. No, it couldn't be empty. We'd never been able to get a Commando out of its shell and I'd have heard if someone had.

That meant there were no spare suits lying around.

There was a chicken in there.

I looked around for some kind of weapon, cursing my decision to leave my shock-stick back at the hotel. I spotted a length of metal pipe and tried to pick it up carefully. As careful as I was, it scraped against the floor and the Commando's head turned towards me, its eyes glowing a bright red.

I moved as fast as I could, swinging towards it before I had a good grip on the pipe. The chicken scrambled away and I hit the floor, dropping my weapon. As I scrabbled to pick it up again the Commando scuttled away. I followed, pipe striking, trying to hit it. But it was dark, even with my torch, and the chicken was a small target.

We skirted past one of the hollowed-out Catchers,

the pipe making it chime like a bell as I once again missed. The Commando leapt into the air and fluttered across the workshop, landing on one of the half-made lasers still in a Catcher's disembodied head. It began fiddling with the lasers and I sprinted across the floor towards it, racing to hit the Commando before it could turn them on.

We drew. The eyes of the Catcher head lit up and glowed red, but I had already reached the Commando, pipe held high over my head, ready to bring it down like a hammer. The Commando had a claw poised over the button that would activate the laser. We stared at each other, eye to glowing eye, daring the other to make the first move.

And that was when Hazel appeared.

Her hair was a mess so she must have just woken up, probably from the racket we'd made. She was rubbing sleep out of her eyes and was wearing a chicken onesie.

"What's going on?" she asked wearily before she'd really seen us. When she did she froze for a moment. Then she got angry.

"Get away from there," she yelled, storming towards us. I thought she was yelling at the chicken but she grabbed the pipe and snatched it out of my hands. I was so surprised I let her have it. Then she turned to the chicken.

"Turn it off," she said in a voice that brooked no argument. It instantly flicked a small lever and the laser's glow faded. "That's better. Are you OK?"

"Yes, thanks, but what—" I started.

"I wasn't talking to you."

I blinked. "You mean is *it* OK? You know this thing?"

"Don't call him a thing," Hazel said angrily. "His name is Clucky."

"Hello," the chicken said.

I stared at it. The voice had definitely come from the ball of metal feathers in front of me. There was no way a ventriloquist had thrown their voice into that thing.

"It can talk?"

"*He. He* can talk. He can talk quite well."

"I don't care if he can recite Shakespeare. Why is he here? Why haven't you got rid of him?"

Hazel muttered something that I couldn't quite grasp.

"What did you say?" I asked her.

"I said, he's my friend." Hazel at least had the decency to look bashful about it. "And he's on our side. We trained with him and he didn't get on that well with the other chickens. Honestly, he was a bit clumsy and they made fun of him. So when the signal went down and everything went crazy we sort of protected him."

I sighed. "Hazel, I know you mean well but you can't trust him. He's probably the spy. He could just be listening to everything we say and reporting it back to his masters."

"Well, that would be dumb," Hazel told me. "Especially seeing as we've only survived this long because of him."

I stared at her, dumbfounded. "What do you mean?" I asked. "Explain."

"Well, you don't really think that just because we spent some time with the chickens we magically know how to operate all their stuff, do you?" Hazel sounded almost amused at the thought. "We weren't much trusted by most of them either. We weren't allowed in the Catchers at any point and of course we never saw a Commando out of his suit. It's impossible."

"What do you mean? Are they bonded to it somehow?"

Hazel frowned. "Sort of. It's kind of hard to explain. They can only get the signal through their suits, and without the signal they're just ordinary chickens."

"Sounds perfect," I said, advancing towards 'Clucky' with hands outstretched. It moved back towards the laser controls.

"Rayna." Hazel put herself firmly between us. "Don't do that. You're frightening him."

"Well, how did you think I was going to react when I found out about this? Did you expect me to be happy?"

"No! Of course I didn't. But I thought Jesse would be here to help me explain."

An icy-cold sensation flooded my spine. "What? What do you mean?"

"Jesse knows. And he's OK with it."

That stopped me. If Hazel was telling the truth, then Jesse must have known about Clucky before he left. And he hadn't mentioned it to me.

He must have known I'd freak out. That wasn't hard to work out. So if Hazel was telling the truth, he must have had a good reason not to tell me. Not just so that I wouldn't freak out but because I didn't need to know. Because it wasn't a danger.

I could trust Jesse about this. But only if Hazel wasn't lying and he really did know.

"Just call him," Hazel was saying. "He'll back me up."

"I would," I said through gritted teeth, "but I tried earlier and got no response. He's probably inside a Catcher right now."

"He's not," said Hazel with utter certainty. "I'd know about it."

"You would, would you? And how...?" I turned towards the chicken as the truth dawned on me. "Oh. So he's your informant. He's not just telling you about how to use the machines."

"That's right," Hazel said. "I told you he was useful."

"But how can his information be up to date? Is he flying between the chickens' headquarters and here? And if he is, how do you know he's not spying on us?"

"He doesn't go to their base. He stays in the building at all times – to avoid reactions like yours. The last thing he wants to do is to fight humans."

"So how does he know everything? How does he know Jesse hasn't been captured?"

Hazel squinted. "The signal that makes them smart also connects them, like a sort of mental internet. It's how the chickens get their orders. They can all share news and stuff on it. I've had him keeping an eye on it for signs that Jesse's been captured ever since he took off. Believe me, once they identified their prisoner, news like that would have got about."

"Why?" I asked. "Is Jesse special somehow?"

Hazel shrugged. "Not particularly. He's about as well known as other members of the council. But they know he helped corrupt the Brotherhood so they'd certainly shout about catching him."

I sighed. "Alright. Let me talk to the thing."

"Be nice," Hazel said, stepping aside and letting me get close to the chicken.

"Will you talk to me?" I asked it.

The chicken just glared at me, scratching the worktop with a metal claw. I think it was threatening me.

"Come on," Hazel said. "Rayna won't hurt you."

"Oh, thank goodness for that. I was all of a flutter," Clucky said. I swear it was being sarcastic.

Hazel ignored this and nodded at him. "Yes. In fact she's going to say sorry for overreacting. She sees now that she was wrong."

"Seriously?" I muttered at my sister out the corner of my mouth. She nodded at me determinedly. "Alright. I'm sorry I got so startled by you. And I'm sorry that I might have overreacted."

I don't think Hazel was very happy with my apology but that was all she was getting. I still wasn't convinced that this chicken was on the side of the angels.

"It's alright," Clucky said. "I'm not up to fowl play."

I just blinked at it. "Was that a joke?" I asked.

"I told you Jesse had been spending time with him," Hazel said, nudging me gently. Then she addressed the chicken again.

"And so, Rayna is going to thank you for everything you've done to help us." Hazel gave me a gentle squeeze on the shoulder as she said this; a gentle squeeze that might just bruise bone.

"No chance," I said. "But I would like some more help now. If that's OK."

The chicken seemed to try and shrug, but instead it made an odd head-bobbing movement. "Alright. What do you need to know?"

"I know you were listening." I felt Hazel glare at me and tried to calm down. "Do you know if Jesse has been captured?"

The chicken shook its head. "I checked recently. There were no reports of anyone being captured near our base in the last few days."

I counted to ten under my breath. It just felt so weird talking to a chicken and I had to constantly throw off the impulse to put a metal bucket over its head. "Can you check again? Just to be sure?"

"Well, if you insist..."

The chicken obviously thought it was a waste of time but it did as I asked anyway. Maybe it just wanted to be friendly. Maybe it just didn't want to get kicked by an angry girl.

It was the sudden stillness that grabbed my attention. The chicken had been bopping this way and that, the way any chicken does when it's not got much to do. Then it suddenly came to a halt, frozen in place. Then it burst into motion, bouncing up and down in the air like an agitated beach ball, wings flailing all over the place.

"What's wrong?" Hazel asked, concerned. I frowned. So this wasn't normal behaviour.

"You've got to go back, you've got to go back," the chicken shrieked.

"What is it talking about?" I asked.

"I don't know. Clucky, can you calm down and talk to us? Who has to go where?"

The chicken's eyes seemed to focus on me. "Her. She's got to go back. To the hotel. She's got to stop it."

"Stop what?" I asked, though I felt that familiar sinking feeling in my stomach. It could really only be one thing.

"The C-800. It's on the move. It's going for its next target."

"Who?" I demanded but I'm not sure it could hear me. It seemed to be disabled by panic and it could only squawk stuff out.

"The hotel... bawk... Get to the hotel... bawk... It's coming... bawk... For the leader."

"Cody?" I asked, shocked. The chicken shook again.

"Not Cody... bawk... Noah."

CHAPTER 16

I've never sprinted as hard as I did to get back from the warehouse to the hotel that morning. I had to stop the next kidnapping. I got there just in time.

The guard was being changed and lots of people with shock-sticks were hanging about. I grabbed a shock-stick from one of them and yelled at the rest.

"We've had news that the Chickenator is coming here. If you see it, try and slow it down. I'm going to find Noah. Stay alert and be careful. Don't do anything stupid. And can someone find Blake? He'll know what to do."

Everyone went scurrying off in different directions and I headed for where Noah should be. I didn't think any of them could beat the Chickenator. But they could at least slow it down. And if its battery really was a problem then the longer it took to find us, the more chance we had of saving Noah.

I ran into Blake in the corridor. I didn't have time to properly explain so I just grabbed him and dragged him along.

"What's going on?" he asked, trying to dig in his heels, but a quick jerk convinced him otherwise.

"Chickenator," I panted, out of breath from the long run. "After Noah. We've got to hurry."

He immediately started sprinting, in a slightly different direction from where the meeting had been yesterday. "He's this way," he called back over his head, "in the communications room. Come on."

As he ran Blake pulled out a whistle from around his neck and started blowing on it. The sharp bursts of sound echoed around the corridors and I could hear the sudden clatter of boots running towards us: his crew had assembled.

We finally arrived at the communications room. I was so wound up and anxious that I was surprised to find the atmosphere in the room so clear and calm. It was the same as usual, just a bunch of people sitting at desks listening to whatever news managed to get through the chickens' firewall.

Noah looked up as we burst through the door. He could tell right away from the expressions on our faces that something was wrong. "What's up?" he asked. "What's gone wrong now?"

"It's the Chickenator," I said, grabbing some chairs and stacking them against the door. "It's here and it's coming for you."

Noah didn't ask if I was sure or how I knew. He just started grabbing the chairs I'd put in front of the door and pulling them away.

"What are you doing?" I asked him. "Are you crazy? We need to lock this place down."

He shook his head and gestured around at the frightened faces. "No. I'm not putting these guys in danger. If it's after me then I'll lead it off and away."

"Noah, you can't do that. It's too fast for you to outrun. I doubt even Billy could do it." Billy was one of the fastest runners in Aberdeen and liked racing Catchers on foot.

"Wait a minute, Rayna. He might have a point."

I turned to Blake and raised my eyebrow questioningly. "What are you talking about?" I asked.

"Well, look at it like this. If we get out of here and everyone in this room barricades themselves in, the Chickenator will have to break through the door to get in. Once it gets in – and let's face it, it will – its limited battery life will force it to go after Noah straight away. If we just stay here, it'll break through our barricade in no time, then it'll capture Noah and still have enough energy to wreck everything we've got."

I could see his logic.

"Alright, let's do this." I turned to the rest of the room. "Once we're gone, lock the door and put everything you can up against it. Do you understand?"

There were a lot of frightened nodding heads and I felt a stab of pity. They didn't want to ever fight a chicken. That's why they'd signed up for communications duty in the first place. I took a moment to curse the chickens for making us all live in fear.

"Come on then," I called, taking Noah by the arm. "Do you have a plan or should we just run blindly through the hotel halls?"

"There's a basement down here where we can hide, and tunnels beyond it. The Chickenator will have to run through most of the hotel to find us. We'll be able to see it coming."

Blake nodded. "Works for me. Look, Rayna, how do you know the Chickenator is after Noah? Is this some other weird test?"

I looked at Blake sidelong. "Believe me, this isn't a test. It's really coming. I've got information that tells me."

I could hear how similar to Hazel I sounded and I quietly chuckled to myself. I still wasn't sure whether I'd tell anyone about Clucky the chicken. No matter what Hazel said or did, I don't think I'd ever fully trust it. But for the moment I had to.

Just then the lights flickered and went out. I stopped and someone ran into me from behind. "Ooof," I said. "Watch where you're going."

"I would," Blake said, "but I can't actually see."

We all dug out our head torches and put them on, lighting the path ahead of us slightly. I'd never known the lights to go off like this before. It was day outside but with no windows the corridors were dark around us. There could only be one answer.

"It's the Chickenator," I muttered. "It's here."

Blake and the rest of his group activated their

shock-sticks, shining their soft blue light around us. I still had the one I'd grabbed in the foyer, and one of Blake's group handed a spare one to Noah. "Here you go." Now we were all armed.

"Let's go," I said, striding towards the nearest stairwell and heading downwards. But before the door had even swung closed behind us, I heard the sound of crashing wood and a scream rent the air. I shuddered. The chicken must have reached the communications room, moving fast after cutting out the lights. It had probably expected the sudden darkness to cause confusion, giving it an advantage. If we hadn't been warned then it would have succeeded. I nodded to myself. It seemed Clucky the chicken had certainly done us a favour.

We reached the bottom of the stairs and headed off. While the layout of the hotel above was logical, the basement was a warren of half-assembled burrows and dead-end corridors.

Noah led the way. "I had the gang working down here in secret," he told me quietly, "while we all still lived in the train station. We knocked in a few walls here and there, to make a secret bunker if we got attacked."

I shushed him into silence. "Good plan but don't talk so loudly." Sound tended to echo underground and I didn't want our position given away.

He nodded and zipped his lips. I smiled at him and made sure we were all sticking close.

Then I noticed one of Blake's group was missing. I hurried up to him. "Have we lost someone already?" I hissed.

Blake snorted. "You're not that observant, are you? I stationed him by the door, so the chicken will have to get past him first."

"Are you sure that's a good idea?" I asked. "Wouldn't it be better if we all faced it together?"

He shook his head. "Nope. If we fight it one at a time we'll slow it down. Each of us will hold it for as long as possible, wearing out its battery and warning the next in line that it's coming. Then when it gets to Noah it'll be weaker and we'll be able to beat it."

In the next moment his words were confirmed. The sound of brave battle cries came bolting down the corridor. I could hear slamming and a frustrated screech that only a chicken could have made. The Chickenator had followed us, and Blake's guy was engaging it.

The fighting went on for long minutes as we hurried on. The battle must have been fierce. But finally the cries and squawks ceased and I knew that Blake's guy must have fallen.

The Chickenator was coming for us.

"Right, formation delta," Blake said as we kept hurrying along. "Hailey and Stuart, hold it off. Everyone else keep quiet or it will hear us. And dim those lights. It might not know which way we've come."

The group must have practised for this moment

because they all spread out in a prearranged formation. Most went to the back and some hurried to the front to cover Noah. Two dropped back and waited in the corridor, extinguishing both their torches and their glowing shock-sticks. Hopefully that would allow them to get the drop on the chicken. As soon as our little bubble of light moved on, they were lost to the darkness. I wished them well but I knew that, just like the guy before them, they weren't there to win, only to stall.

Everything was quiet as we hurried along, slower than before now that our lights were dimmed. The Chickenator came across the next group after a few minutes, just as we were ducking through a hole someone had hacked into the wall. The screams of battle echoed eerily around us as we pressed forward. I shivered, not liking to think how it must feel to stand there in the dark, knowing that something was coming for you – something you couldn't beat.

"Hailey and Stuart should hold it off for a while," Blake whispered. "They've got some surprises planned."

Blake was right. I swore I could hear something like firecrackers echoing around me.

But the ferocious noise of their heroic stand died eventually and I knew that once again we were being tracked. Blake had already nodded to another member of the group. "You're up, Angus. Bet you only last five minutes."

Angus snorted. "If I last any less than ten I owe you some chocolate."

"Done." Blake clapped him on the shoulder and started walking. Angus stopped by the hole in the wall, arm raised and shock-stick glowing merrily. I guessed he planned to ambush the chicken as it came through.

Again the darkness swallowed him as we hurried along, but all too soon we heard yelling behind us. I frowned, trying to make out what Angus was saying over the clanks of battering metal. He appeared to be singing along with the fight. I shook my head. I will say it once again: completely crazy.

"Angus likes singing in a fight. Says it gives him rhythm," Blake explained.

"Is that so?" Noah replied casually, while his eyes darted all over the walls. "What's he singing right now?"

I paused for a second, cocking my head to the side and listening. "Chick, chick, chick, chick, chicken. Lay a little egg for me."

Noah's teeth gleamed white in the darkness when he grinned.

CHAPTER 17

Angus managed to hold that wall for fifteen minutes. Fifteen minutes while we hurried deeper and deeper through the labyrinth of underground tunnels. I wasn't sure if the chicken could even catch us up at this point. Surely its battery must be getting low? Maybe Angus would hold and we'd be able to escape?

The layout of the underground tunnels did odd things to the sound around us. At times it sounded like we were miles away from the fighting. At others they could have been right around the corner. So when Angus's voice finally fell silent I wondered if we'd just moved out of range. Blake obviously thought the same thing because he held up his hand, motioning us to a stop. We paused and looked at him. He backtracked a bit, listened for a while then came hurrying back. With a sharp gesture he ushered us forward.

He didn't say anything, but I could tell by the grave expression on his face: Angus had fallen.

We came to a crossroads where a number of tunnels snaked away in different directions.

"Connie. Andrea. Good luck." At Blake's words the last two people watching our backs slipped away. They moved down different corridors and stood, crouched and ready. They didn't extinguish their torches or shock-sticks. They obviously meant to confuse the chicken, make it wonder which way we'd gone. I hurried on with the others, looking back and hoping their tactic would work.

There were only five of us now: Noah, Blake, myself, and the two guarding Noah from the front. I began to feel hopeful as we walked for a while hearing nothing behind us. Maybe the chicken had got lost. Maybe it had left to recharge. It must have been chasing us for more than an hour and we'd been holding it back at every moment we could. Surely it wouldn't have much more power?

But before my hopes could be raised too far I heard yells behind us and knew that the last of our rear guards had engaged the enemy.

"It's just us now," Blake muttered and lengthened his stride. "Let's put some distance between us and that beast."

As the sounds of fighting wore on, we charged ahead, sprinting now.

And then suddenly the Chickenator was in front of us.

Maybe it knew a better route through the underground maze. Maybe it was just too fast for us. Whatever, it didn't really matter at this point. All that mattered was that it was there, ahead of us, its chest cavity already open and waiting.

That would probably have been the end of Noah if not for his two guards. He was running too fast to stop; even as I watched him try I knew he wouldn't be able to. He would run straight into that dark hollow, then it would snap shut and he'd be gone. But instead of slowing down, his guards accelerated, their head torches blossoming into bright burning light. The chicken recoiled from the sudden glare, flinching away. One of the guards leapt forward, planting both feet in a flying kick that snapped into the chicken's chest. He rolled away as his partner backed him up, swinging his shock-stick.

The chicken was driven back, trying desperately to close its chest. I thought that would be it; that would be how we'd defeat it. But before I could call out, the Chickenator had already acted, slamming its chest shut. I could hear bolts shifting behind its chest plate, locking it into place. The chance was lost. Now we'd just have to fight it the old-fashioned way.

The two guards, probably brothers or old best friends, stood side by side. By our bad luck or the chicken's good planning, we'd been caught in a wide section of tunnel, making it hard to block the way to Noah.

"Come on," Blake growled as he ran forward to reinforce the line. I joined him. I looked behind me and held out a hand to stop Noah following. He stopped, though he didn't look happy about it. I guess I'd have felt the same if I was stopped from helping the people defending me.

"We can hold it off a little bit longer. Come on, you bucket of fried chicken! Are you just going to stand there or are we going to dance?" yelled Blake.

We formed a tight wedge, our shock-sticks blazing, as the Chickenator rushed us. It seemed slightly slower this time and I was sure I could see nicks and dents in its armour that hadn't been there before. Obviously the fight hadn't gone all its own way. Getting this far had cost it, maybe dearly, just as we'd hoped it would. Of course that just made it even more desperate to get its prize.

In my head I could hear a little clock ticking, counting down the seconds or minutes until the chicken would have to pull out. It had to factor in the time it would take to get back to the Catchers, who were probably waiting outside to transport the Chickenator back to their headquarters. That had to be soon. We just had to hold it at bay.

And we were managing. The tunnel might have been wide compared to others but it was still narrow enough to limit the chicken's options. It couldn't go around us and it couldn't go over. So it had to go through us. And every time it tried, it met the glowing force of our shock-sticks. Blake snarled and fought, either flinging insults at it or giving us advice.

"Time your strikes, people. If we hit it together, we hurt it."

Again and again it charged, and again and again we held it back. We worked as a team, some of us blocking its strikes, while others attacked. Blake was right: it could clearly feel the impact of four shock-sticks at the same time, even through its armour.

Finally it stopped, and just stood there, looking at us with oddly questioning eyes. Our head torches and shock-sticks lit it brightly. Standing there like that, totally fearless, it struck me how weird it was that we were fighting a giant metal chicken, painted black with mad green eyes. It was beautifully made and well formed. Even though I hated it I could admire the craftsmanship that had gone into making it.

Blake growled, "Either fight us or run away. We can do this all day."

The chicken stared at us for a moment longer, obviously considering its next move. I imagined the little live chicken in the cockpit of the machine, looking at all the gauges, assessing the damage and figuring out a way around us. Maybe it was checking the power levels and realising it couldn't go on any longer.

Finally it came to a decision. It turned away and sped off into the darkness.

There was a quick quiet moment of shock. I don't believe any of us actually thought it was gone. Surely this was some trick. We couldn't be that lucky. Could we?

Eventually we began to give a ragged cheer. The thing

wasn't coming back. We'd done it. We'd driven it off. Noah was safe.

Then came the sound of footsteps, impossibly fast. Closer and closer they got, and staring into the darkness I was able to make out two rapidly approaching green glowing lights: its eyes.

"Brace yourselves," Blake roared.

We scrambled together and stood firm, shoulder to shoulder, shock-sticks held out before us.

Which did no good whatsoever. The chicken just ploughed through us all, not even slowing down, its wings held out in front of it like enormous shields. I felt a juddering down my arms as I was thrown back and realised that my shock-stick had broken.

I lay there, stunned and unable to move. The edges of my vision grew black but I wasn't sure if I was about to fall unconscious or if my head torch had just been broken.

Then the chicken loomed over me. It seemed to limp slightly and one look at its face told me it was angry. More than angry it was furious that we'd made it fight so hard. Children.

A small smile creased my lips. That was a start: one small victory.

It bent over me, its beak raised viciously. I realised it was about to strike me and I knew that would hurt. It might even break one of my arms. I'd be stuck in the hospital, in incredible pain and unable to fight against the chickens. That was possibly the worst thing it could do to me. I tried to roll away but the blow had knocked me silly. Even with all my effort I couldn't get my arms to move.

I was defenceless.

The Chickenator looked me right in the eye, forcing me to connect with those strange green lights. Then it very deliberately raised its clawed foot and held it above my leg.

"Stop." The voice came from behind me and, though I couldn't see him, I recognised the voice as Noah's. He walked forwards into my field of view and placed a hand against the chicken, pushing it firmly backwards.

No! I tried to scream out. But the words wouldn't come. *Don't do this, Noah. Start running. If I distract it, you can still get away. Run and hide and leave me to my fate.*

But Noah wouldn't do it. Noah couldn't do it. That's why he'd managed, despite not being a great fighter, to become the leader of one of the largest groups in Aberdeen; and why he'd maintained enough power to check Cody when he went too far. Noah was compassionate and Noah cared. He was about as able to walk away from helping someone as he was able to fly.

"You're here for me. Well, you've got me. Just take me without hurting any of the others. I won't even struggle. I promise."

The chicken looked at Noah and its chest slid open. It wasn't the smooth slide I'd seen before. No doubt about it, we'd damaged it. That was something to hold on to. Noah took a step towards the Chickenator and turned around, preparing to back into it.

"N-n-n-n-n..." I said, trying to say his name, but I felt like a computer that had suffered an unexpected shutdown. My programmes hadn't finished loading up yet. Some of them hadn't even started.

He knew what I was trying to say. He looked down at me and smiled.

"Take care, Rayna. And keep up the fight." Then he stepped backwards and the chest closed over his face. The chicken glared at me, raised one leg then turned and sped away. In a moment it was gone.

I lay still on the floor, unable to move and not wanting to. That was it. We'd failed.

Another council member, and one of my closest friends, Noah, had been taken.

CHAPTER 18

Council meetings these days sucked. Every one just signalled that something else had gone wrong. The empty spaces around the table spoke of those we'd lost. So far we'd only been able to replace Jeremy. Kyle now sat on the council, looking around nervously. He'd make a good replacement. He'd basically been doing the job even when Jeremy was around, making sure everyone had the supplies they needed. But no one had come forward to fill the other vacant positions. I wasn't surprised. With four council members taken in as many days, they'd just be making themselves a target.

For once Cody was late. Around me sat Deborah, Blake, Kyle and Hazel. We didn't say much, just stared at the table. I don't know about them but I was trying to figure out who was the spy and who'd get taken next.

When Cody finally turned up he got right to the point. He sat down, Percy standing behind him as usual, looked at us and said, "I'm taking over as leader."

We all stared at him for a moment. Then Deborah

raised a hand. "Does that mean I don't have to be here any more?" she asked.

Cody nodded.

"Fantastic. I'll be with my patients. Let me know what happens." Then she stood up and left.

I looked at the others, aghast. "Are you all OK with this? He's taking over."

Blake shrugged. "I just take orders anyway. Makes no difference to me."

Kyle nodded. "I'd feel more comfortable with it, honestly."

"Hazel?"

"Doesn't matter if I like it or not. You never listen to me anyway."

Cody smiled. "Great, now that we've got that sorted let's get down to business. Blake, what can you tell me about fighting the Chickenator?"

I looked on, amazed, as Blake recounted the story. Did that really just happen? I'd expected Cody to try something like this. He'd never made his desire to lead a secret. But I'd expected some resistance. I'd expected him to have to do more than just say he was leader.

"I definitely think we were close to beating it," Blake finished up. "A small, enclosed space so it can't move about much, and tougher weapons."

"You don't think running would be a good idea?" Hazel looked at Blake intently, all business. He shook his head.

"No, I think we did the best we could in those

tunnels. It's too fast to outrun. It wasn't familiar with the terrain and we were able to hold it up and do some damage. Those were as close to ideal conditions as you can get and they weren't enough. We need to attack in a confined space in formation with better weapons."

"Alright. Hazel, you said the Brotherhood has been working on new weapons to take it down. How's that going?"

"It's been a day," she told Cody frankly. "We're working as fast as we can but it'll be at least two more before we have anything to share."

She hesitated then said to him, "You do know they'll be going after you now, right? If you've just declared yourself as our supreme leader then you've just moved to the top of their list."

"I know." Cody's face was perfectly calm. "And I'm counting on it."

Hazel hesitated again. "Alright, then I'll try and get some personalised weapons for you and Percy. That might help."

Percy grinned. "Make mine big and sparky."

"I'll see what I can do."

As if working his way down a list, Cody turned to Blake. "What's the state of our army and defences?"

"Defences?"

"Yes. If there was a full-scale chicken attack and they threw everything they could at us, how would we handle it?"

Blake rubbed his head. "Right now? Probably not

very well. The Chickenator put all my best guys in hospital. They'll be out soon, but they're no use to us right now. And we need them."

"You have at least a few days," Hazel said calmly.

Blake looked at her, surprised. "Yeah?" he asked.

"By the sound of it, you did that chicken some serious damage. They'll have to fix it up, which will take a while. Trust me." Hazel directed that last statement at me. She must have heard it from Clucky.

"Alright then," said Blake. "Well, the only thing that could really stop an army of chickens if they came flying in would be lasers, but we don't have many set up. The Brotherhood warehouse is probably better defended than this place or the power plant."

"That's not good." Cody made a few notes on a piece of paper and turned to Hazel. "Do you have more lasers?"

"Yes, a lot. We've been trying to put them on wheels to make them portable, but we haven't succeeded yet."

"Well, forget about that for the moment. I want them mounted on buildings that we can hide in."

"Alright. Just this hotel?"

"No." Finally Cody turned to me. "What will we need to fire up the GPS satellite locator?"

"The one we got from Robert Gordon's?"

"Of course. What other GPS satellite locator do we have?"

I took a breath and ignored the sarcasm. "Well, it has to be positioned somewhere high and have access to signals. Then you just turn it on and it automatically finds a satellite to target."

"Right." Cody motioned to Percy, who handed him a map. He looked over it for a moment before tapping it with his finger. "There are some tenement flats at the beach. Can you set the GPS and lasers up in a top flat there?"

Hazel, Blake and I nodded.

"Good. Now that we've got that gadget, and sacrificed Glen in the process, we need to use it. I want it broadcasting as soon as possible and I don't want any chicken to disrupt it. If this really is a testing ground, then the Chickenator will be heading after world leaders next. The Allies could use that information. They might even be so grateful that they send a rescue party for us. Stranger things have happened. Install lots of lasers on the building to protect the GPS, and we'll all bunk down there. We'll also need an escape plan. I'll figure that out and circulate the plans. I'll also elect someone to take over from Sally. Rayna, you're in charge of Communications for now. Kyle, gather enough supplies to last a week. Anything else we need to talk about?"

Hazel looked at me beseechingly. She must be worried that I'd bring up Clucky and expose her. I still wasn't sure what to do about that, so I just shrugged at her and kept my mouth shut. She smiled at me gratefully.

Cody glowered at us and nodded. "OK. Well then, you've got jobs to do. Go and do them."

Blake, Hazel, Kyle and Percy left. Once the door had swung shut Cody looked up at me. "Is there a problem?" he asked.

"You won't get away with this," I told him simply. "You may be in control for now but it won't last."

He was round the table in a moment, standing before me, staring into my eyes.

I couldn't help myself: I shivered.

"You think I'm doing this just because I want to be in charge?" he said, his voice barely ruffled by emotion. I swallowed.

"Yes."

"Well, you're right." He turned away and paced around the table. "We'll be better off if I lead us. There's barely any point in arguing about it. But that's not the only reason. Do you remember that graph I showed you? And remember I said people would get scared?"

"You said that in six months we'd all split up and go back into hiding."

"Well, that was before a Chickenator decided to start pecking up all our leaders. Right now I'd be surprised if we had weeks."

"What? I mean things are bad, but they're not *that* bad."

"It waltzed in here, Rayna. Right into our headquarters. And you know how highly people thought of Noah. They're scared, and if one more of us gets taken, I think we'll be finished. We need to take it out. We need to show everyone in Aberdeen that we're strong enough to handle anything the chickens throw at us."

I'd been running all over the place for the past few days and I hadn't really hung out with any other kids. I tried to remember if the people I'd passed in corridors had seemed more stressed than normal. I think they had.

I said the first thing that came to mind: "And you're the one it'll come for."

He smiled slightly. "Yes, which is good for us. It means we know where it'll be heading."

"So that's your plan? You're acting as bait?"

"Kind of. But I don't want to be grabbed any time soon. I'll keep a low profile for a few days, while we get prepared. Only council members will know where I am. Then by the time it finds me we'll be ready: we'll have lasers up and running, Blake and all his chicken hunters will be armed to the teeth, and we'll jump it."

"But the spy will probably just tell them where you're hiding."

He shrugged. "There's not a lot I can do about that, other than get everything set up quickly. As far as I can see, it'll either be you, Blake or Hazel. And you're all key to the plan."

"Do you really think I could be the spy?"

"Do you think I could be?" My silence was enough to tell him that I did. "Then you've no right to be offended."

"And if you get caught?" Cody must have a Plan B.

Unless he didn't care what happened to us after he was taken.

"Use the GPS satellite locator, contact everyone out there. Tell them about the Chickenator. The chickens won't like you transmitting that data so they'll try and stop you. You, Blake and Hazel will have to round up some guys to operate the lasers and you'd better do it fast before the chickens cut our power off..."

I stared at Cody. "You really have thought of everything."

He nodded. "I've tried. Now you've got a job to do. Get that communicator set up and ready. I'll see you in a few days – hopefully."

He walked towards to the door.

I nodded and saluted, only half sarcastically.

"Yes, Cody," I said.

CHAPTER 19

A few days later, the councillors met Cody at the tenement flats by the sea.

"So you're still with us," I said, secretly pleased to have our new leader at the helm of the operation.

Cody shrugged. "So far so good. We're out of the way and well protected. Right now I've got enough lasers around me to take down a fleet of Catchers." He had to yell to be heard over the sound of hammering coming from outside.

Cody had set up an office in the flats. A fast flood of paper was quietly flowing across his desk. I'm not sure where it all came from – we didn't usually write much down – but Cody seemed to sustain it somehow. He would probably make a scary lawyer or something when he grew up.

A laser was even being fitted inside the room, one of the many that should keep the giant robotic Catchers off our backs while we were sending the signal. Hazel was installing this one herself, probably so fewer people knew where Cody was.

The building was heavily guarded, to protect the satellite locator and prevent surprise attacks. But Blake and Percy had been told to guard just Cody himself. I knew Percy was looking forward to trying out his new toys.

"Check these out, Ambassador." Percy was brandishing a pair of gloves, gauntlets really, made of metal, glinting in the light from the window. After hearing how Percy had gone down punching a Catcher, the Brotherhood had tailor-made these for him. "They're like shock-sticks for punching."

"Those look awesome," I replied, genuinely impressed by the Brotherhood's skills.

"The signal defences are almost complete," Blake said, standing tall to present his information to Cody. I think he liked to consider himself a soldier with Cody as his general. "Most of the lasers are in place and the rest will be ready in a few hours. The safe room that you asked for has been built, as well as we could manage. Kyle has filled it with supplies so you could hide out there for a while without going hungry. We've also reinforced the power station with spare lasers."

Cody nodded in a business-like way. "That was good thinking," he said. "And we'll have enough power to run them all?"

"We should; all our tests have been going well until now. Of course, we can't be sure until we actually try to power everything at once."

"Fine." Cody looked out the window at the sun setting in the distance. "And the GPS satellite locator?"

I shrugged. "It's set up but I don't know if it works. If you're right and it draws in a ton of Catchers, I'd rather wait until all our lasers are operational before we try it."

Just then there was a knock at the door. We looked at each other suspiciously. Cody had given express orders that he was not to be disturbed. I didn't know who would dare to annoy him. He'd been scary enough before he ran all of Aberdeen.

Percy looked through the peephole to see who was outside. His face went white and he stumbled backwards. Then there was a massive thud and the door came flying into the room.

In the empty doorway stood the Chickenator, one foot raised after kicking the door in. With slow, measured steps it started strutting forward.

"How does it keep finding us?" I yelled as we all scrambled into defensive positions. "No one else knew we were here."

"Shut up and get ready to fight," Percy snarled at me.

Four of us went to meet our adversary. Blake led the way, staff crackling in his hand. I stood next to him, quietly watching his back, gripping my shock-stick uncertainly.

Percy strode forward, an ugly grin on his face, smashing his fists together. Sparks glowed and then fell like dying stars to the ground. He looked like he was going to enjoy this.

Beside him was Cody. I wanted to tell him not to fight, but the look on his face told me there would be no stopping him. He had a brand new baton, smaller and easier to wield than a cumbersome shock-stick; it would allow him to move quickly and keep himself defended.

As he proved in the next minute when the chicken darted forward, chest opening. It obviously didn't want to be drawn into an extended fight. It looked as if it had been partially repaired, but not fully finished. It didn't move with quite the same agility as before. It was fast, but Cody was just as fast, if not faster; he must have been training with Percy. He swayed to the side, rolling away and lashing out with his baton at the same time. There was a sharp crack and I thought I saw the chicken stagger, then Percy came bounding in.

"Go for the chest, Percy," Blake barked out, moving in as well. "Just like we planned."

Percy grunted and launched himself at the chicken's open chest cavity. It tried to close the hatch but Percy was in the way. He sent punch after punch pounding into its insides and the chicken rocked.

It back-pedalled, its feet skittering about as it struggled to regain its balance. It managed to shake off Percy and snap its chest shut. It steadied itself, about to move forward, but Blake took some ball bearings from his pouch and threw them in its path. The chicken hit them and skidded, struggling to stay on its feet. Percy surged forward and punched it a couple more times.

I held my breath. If we kept attacking and didn't let it recover, we might actually be able to beat the Chickenator. We might win.

The Chickenator obviously realised that too. It turned and leapt, soaring over the desk and landing on the other side. Papers scattered everywhere. I thought I heard a squeak and my thoughts turned to Hazel. She'd been working on the laser just over there. Had she managed to get out? Then I saw a small hand poking out from beneath the desk. No, she was still there, hiding.

Ignore her, I silently commanded the chicken. *She's not a threat. Let her be.* "Shore up, guys," I murmured. "Let's take this slowly and carefully."

The chicken paused for a while, maybe planning its next move. I savoured the brief respite and regained my breath.

"Well?" Cody asked. "Are we having a tea break?"

"I'll bring the biscuits," Percy replied and Blake barked out a laugh. I didn't respond, just watched the Chickenator's eyes. They glimmered and the bird looked furious but it stayed still, maybe trying to stare us out.

But we couldn't just stand there forever. We edged forward, keeping Cody in the centre of the group. The chicken let us come and I felt a flash of misgiving.

Then it bounded forward and the fight was on.

It headed for Blake this time, which was a surprise. We'd all been expecting the first move to be against Cody but obviously we were wrong. Maybe that was what it was counting on. We were slower to react and Blake only just managed to duck a buffeting wing. I moved to Blake's side as Percy moved to the other. The chicken's body seemed to shiver as it dodged a few of Percy's punches and moved further away from me and Blake. Then it spun round and darted for Cody. Instead of rolling out of the way again he just dropped down to his knees. The chicken flew straight over his head and almost crashed into the opposite wall. We advanced behind it, Percy in the centre, Blake to the left, me to the right and Cody getting to his feet behind us. The chicken jinked and tried to get past us but Percy punched it again and it bobbed back down.

"Keep it contained, guys. Slow and steady," Blake told us.

Then it broke to the side, skirting round Blake and hitting him with a flap of its wing. He took it on the shoulder and spun round, landing on the ground but still conscious. I ran towards the chicken, shock-stick blazing but it accepted the hit and pushed past me. As I stumbled I saw Percy move forward, Cody a little behind. The chicken threw out another wing, but instead of dodging it Percy caught it and held tight. Sparks flared along the wing tip as the chicken tried to flap away, but Percy wouldn't budge.

"Now, Blake," he called and Blake rose up behind

the chicken. Taking his shock-stick in both hands, he swung it with all his might at the back of the chicken's head.

There was a bright disorientating flash as his stick connected and broke, and electricity streaked across the chicken's body. It gave a shriek and Percy was forced to let go.

I looked down, backing away and blinking rapidly, trying to regain focus. I heard a grunt and looked up, hardly daring to hope.

But there was no point. The chicken was still standing. It moved slower than before, but it hadn't been knocked out like we'd hoped it would be.

"OK. That didn't work." Blake grabbed another shock-stick from a rack in the corner, snapping it on with a faint hiss. "Plan B."

As far as I was aware, we didn't have a Plan B.

The Chickenator threw a kick at Percy, which sent him spinning into Blake as it stalked towards Cody. The chicken had the measure of the fight now, and it brimmed with confidence.

Cody backed towards the desk, ball bearings clacking together under his feet. The chicken suddenly darted round, getting between him and the desk. Cody instinctively hurled himself away from it and into a wall.

I ran forward but it felt like I was moving through treacle. I wouldn't get there in time. The Chickenator would gobble up Cody then fall backwards through the window and glide away. There was no way we'd get Cody back.

Then a figure moved behind the chicken and there was a sudden smell of ozone. It arched its back, sparks crawling across its body. After a second they shut off and the Chickenator crashed to the floor. The lights in it eyes stopped glowing and it lay still.

I looked up at the figure, and Hazel looked back at me, smiling slightly.

"How?" I asked.

She held up a cable, which had been intended to power the room's laser.

"I plugged it into the mains."

I rushed to her and was about to give her a hug when there was a sudden yell from outside and a laser burst lit up the night sky. A dark shape loomed up and I had to pull Hazel away from the enraged Catcher that suddenly smashed its head through the window.

There was a blur of black as the back of the Chickenator popped open and the chicken inside darted across the room and into the Catcher's throat. With a squawk it fell backwards and flew away.

"Plug that laser in, Hazel," I said, a cold feeling creeping through my bones. "They're coming."

"But we haven't tried transmitting anything yet," Cody said, clambering back to his feet.

"That's not what they're after. The C-800 is taken everywhere by at least five Catchers. They don't want to lose the prototype." As Hazel explained, I gave the empty Chickenator a kick.

Then we heard more yelling, and flashes lit up the window behind me as the Catchers appeared.

"They won't stop until they've got it back," Hazel finished.

Everyone seemed to freeze in panic for a moment before Cody snapped into action.

"We can't let them have it back," he said simply. "Retreat to the safe room on the ground floor and take that thing with us. Hazel, keep on that laser until we're out of the room, then come and join us. Percy, grab the Chickenator and we'll drag it downstairs with us. Rayna and Blake, power up the lasers on the floors below. We're three floors up, people, and we need to get down. Let's move out."

Everyone scrambled into action, Hazel firing at any Catchers that got too near. I darted down the stairs with Blake while Cody helped Percy with the Chickenator.

The stairs seemed to fly by beneath me as I hurried down them, bouncing off the wall at the bottom and straight through the door of the second-floor flat. I could see the laser positioned by the window.

I got to it and flicked the switch, turning it on. Above me I could hear Hazel blasting away and see the long red beam of her weapon.

"Are you OK here?" Blake asked and I nodded.

"Yeah, go start up the laser downstairs. The more guns we've got firing the better."

He clapped me on the shoulder and was away.

Even though the building was covered with lasers there weren't that many people about to fire them. Yet again, the Chickenator must have taken out all the guards before heading inside to attack us. The Catchers were flying round the building, dark shapes flitting here and there. The one that had taken the Chickenator pilot seemed to have disappeared. Hazel had hit another, clipping its wing and sending it spiralling to the ground. But that still left three.

It was down to two by the time Hazel appeared at my shoulder. Blake's beam had shot out from the first floor, catching one of the chickens by surprise. After losing a leg, it turned round and got out of there.

"Rayna, time to go. Down another floor."

I sent a last shot winging at a chicken then turned and sprinted out of the apartment. Hazel by my side, we flashed down the stairs. I reached the ground-floor laser just in time to shoot up at a Catcher that was diving for Blake.

That left one. I had it in my sights and pulled the trigger. I just missed but it flew away anyway. It must have given up.

I sighed, happy that we'd driven them back, and my exhausted hand slipped from the laser gun.

Which, of course, was when the Catcher rose in front of me and cannoned through the window.

Hazel and I were thrown back, sprawled on the floor. The Catcher Hazel had hit at the start of the fight loomed above us. Its wing was hanging off and it didn't look like it could fly. I looked around desperately, searching for an escape route. But the chicken was too close; we'd never be able to outrun it.

Shakily I got to my feet. If I was going to be pecked up I wanted to be standing tall, looking the chicken right in its beak.

It grinned at me, cockily assured of its victory. I pulled the shock-stick from my belt, gave it an experimental swing or two.

"Come get me, you walking pillow."

I took a deep breath and the world slowed down. The chicken's eyes gleamed evilly. Its open mouth glinted and I thought I could see all the way down its throat.

Then Hazel charged into me, knocking me out of the way.

I landed heavily, the shock-stick spinning from my hand. I was defenceless.

"What are you doing?" I yelled.

"Getting you out of the way," she muttered.

The chicken turned towards us, slightly confused but greedily anticipating being able to eat two of us. Then with a flash of red light its left leg disappeared. It fell to the ground, flapping in surprise. Another flash and a wing fell off, the hinge connecting it to the body melting away under the laser.

A figure appeared round the side of the chicken, my fallen laser in his hand. He spun, long coat flapping behind him, raking a long gash in the chicken's side and taking off the other leg in the process. Then he raised the laser to the immobilised chicken's head.

"Time to fry," he called and I felt my heart leap.

There was a clattering as the Catcher's head fell off. It rolled towards the hole in the window and something blasted off. The chicken inside must have activated the emergency ejector.

But I didn't care. My attention was on the person in front of me. He dropped the laser with a loud clank and turned towards me. For the first time, I looked up at him instead of down as he stood over me and offered his hand.

"Hiya, Rayna," Jesse said, grin in its usual position on his face. "Sorry I'm late."

CHAPTER 20

I stared up at Jesse for a moment, trying to make sense of the situation.

Jesse shouldn't be here. Jesse was off somewhere in Aberdeenshire. He'd been captured.

"Rayna?" he asked, concerned. "Are you OK?"

Slowly, I walked towards him, mouth slightly open. He smiled at me as I raised my hand...

...and punched him in the arm as hard as I could.

He stumbled backwards, smile fading. "Ow, that hurt. What was that for?"

I followed him, trying to get close enough to hit him again, but he kept retreating. "What for? What for? I thought you'd been captured. I thought I'd never see you again. And yet you turn up here..." I took a deep breath. Hazel was trying to get between us. "Why didn't you radio me? I've been worried sick."

"How worried?"

"She broke into the Brotherhood's warehouse in the middle of the night," Hazel chimed in.

Jesse looked impressed. "That's worried."

"Jesse!"

"It wasn't my fault." He pulled out his walkie-talkie and tossed it to me. I caught it automatically. "It ran out of charge and there's no power out there. I couldn't recharge it."

"Oh." That made sense. I hadn't thought of that. "Sorry for punching you."

"Don't mention it. It's nice to know you care..." he rubbed his arm, "...I think. Hey, if you broke into their warehouse did you find anything... interesting?"

"Yes, I know about Clucky," I told him. "I've not decided what to do about him yet."

"Don't do anything," Hazel and Jesse both said at the same time. I looked at them, eyebrows raised.

"Trust me," Jesse said.

"Fine."

"Cool. So have I missed much around here? Have you caught the spy yet?"

I shook my head then nodded deeper into the tenement. "Not yet. Look, we'd better go report back to Cody, see if they're OK. And you'd better tell them what you've learned."

"Alright." We walked off, Jesse trailing behind me, asking questions.

"So did the thing that took Sally come bawk?"

I ignored the chicken sound. "Yes, actually. Turns out it's a specialist kidnapper robot. It pursues its target, smashing through all resistance until it gets it."

"Huh. Sounds scary. What did you call it?"

"The Chickenator."

"Nice."

"Thought you'd appreciate it."

"So who did it take?" Jesse tried to sound casual as he asked, but I could hear the tension in his voice.

"Jeremy first, then Glen. Noah got taken a few days ago."

"Oh." Jesse paused for a moment and, looking back, I saw his shoulders slump. "Do we have a plan for dealing with it?"

"Already done. It came for Cody, and Hazel managed to take it out. That's why all those Catchers were attacking. They were trying to get it back. Hopefully they didn't manage to."

"Good. Wait, if Sally, Glen, Noah and Jeremy have all been taken then who's on the council now?"

"No one really," I said, kicking a door at the end of a corridor. Only the bottom half of the door opened, probably some sort of defence Cody had thought up. Hazel and I had to duck; Jesse just walked right under it. "Cody's taken over. I think he's done it for the right reasons though."

"Huh," Jesse frowned. "So, long story short, the Chickenator managed to get half the council but Cody survived and he's now in charge. There's still a spy out there somewhere and the chickens are likely to attack again, trying to get their robot back?"

"That's about it."

"Alright."

There didn't seem to be any evidence of chickens on our way to the safe room. Ahead of us Blake poked his head round a door. He did a double take when he saw Jesse.

"What are you doing here?" he asked.

"Do we like him now?" Jesse asked under his breath.

"About fifty-fifty," I replied. Raising my voice, I called back to Blake, "He turned up at the perfect time. Is everyone OK?"

"No chickens managed to get this far," Blake called back. He seemed disappointed. "And we've still got the Chickenator."

"They must have lacked the quill to win."

Blake looked at Jesse for a moment then grinned.

"They were out of their league. Now they're down and out."

Jesse nodded, appreciating the pun. "It must have been an egg-citing time for you."

"Oh, it was cracking."

"It was pretty exciting for me too. I started having fun as soon as I crested the stairs."

I looked back and forth between them, as if I was watching a tennis match.

"So you just appeared un-egg-spectedly? I'm impressed you were able to wing it."

"I've always been a clutch player."

I ground the palm of my hand into my forehead. Beside me Hazel was looking at the two of them, amused. "Alright, you two, that's enough. You're both very funny. Can we get on with it and find Cody?"

Blake winked at Jesse. "I could have out-punned you, you know."

"We'll have a rematch sometime. I'll put that idea to nest."

"Jesse!"

"Sorry, Rayna." He looked at me and grinned. We all walked together into the safe room.

I guess I was expecting something grand from Cody's hideaway but it was just a room with a table. A laser was mounted directly in front of the door, ready for whatever came through it, glowing red. We quickly ducked out of the way as Percy unplugged it. The Chickenator sat slumped in the corner, like a discarded doll. Hazel wandered over and began fiddling with it.

"What sort of weapons will you be able to make out of that?" Blake asked her. I noticed he was being more friendly than usual. I suppose taking down the Chickenator had earned his respect.

"Probably nothing," Hazel said absentmindedly. "There are no lasers. I guess the wings could be used as shields but we could probably make those anyway. I'd like to take it back to headquarters to investigate it further."

"Fine," Cody said before turning to us. "I see that you've made it back, Jesse."

"Yes, Cody. It's nice to know you missed me."

Cody gave his wintry smile. "I didn't say that. Now what did you learn?"

Everyone looked at Jesse expectantly. He smiled back.

"I'm not telling you," he said.

A small frown creased Cody's forehead and I groaned. Trust Jesse to be difficult.

"Jesse, things changed while you were away. I'm in charge now. So tell me what you learned."

"No, I don't care that you're the leader. I've got a plan and part of it is not telling *you*."

"Do I even want to know what you're wittering on about?" Cody asked.

"It can't hurt," Percy said, giving his opinion for once.

"Fine," Cody gestured at Jesse. "Go on then."

"There's a chicken in the room and I don't mean our robotic friend in the corner. We all know it. One of us is a traitor."

We all glanced at each other quickly and then back at Jesse. "That's why I can't go into details of my plan. I can only go over the outline. But basically we're going to bust everyone out of the chickens' prison."

There was an awed hush.

"Maybe you can risk a few more details," I told him.

"Alright. Rayna and I will lead a team out of the city. At a predetermined time you will cause a diversion that will draw all the Catchers to you. Then we'll take advantage of the lack of guards and free the prisoners. Easy."

"That's an incredibly dumb plan," Cody said. "How could we lure all the Catchers into attacking us?"

"You can broadcast something," Hazel said from the corner. "That was your plan, right? That if things got bad you would start sending information to the Allies and fight off the chickens when they came for you. Well, they've already tried to break in here once. If they're serious next time, they'll probably send everything they can."

"And if they do, we could easily be overwhelmed. Besides," and here Cody lowered his voice slightly, "I'm guessing that it's not just kids held captive there? There are adults as well?"

Jesse nodded. "From what I could see, yes."

"Well then, do we really want them to come back?"

"What do you mean, Cody?" I asked. "Of course we want them back."

"I'm just saying, we're doing alright by ourselves. We have a solid position here. If the adults come back they'll change things. Besides, we might get into trouble."

"Trouble?" Hazel looked puzzled. "For what? We've done nothing wrong."

Percy coughed. "We've destroyed quite a lot of Aberdeen. And stolen stuff. And set some stuff on fire. And stolen stuff then set it on fire. They're not going to be too happy about all that."

"Well... we were fighting a war. They'll understand." Even as he was saying it I could see doubt on Jesse's face.

"Depends what they find out about," Percy muttered, but Jesse breezed on.

"Look, we need the grown-ups. You know we need them. Don't you miss your parents? Even if they are slightly mad about some of the stuff that's happened, I think they'll understand; it was self-defence."

"Alright, alright." Cody called the meeting back to attention. "What will you need for your plan to work?"

"A team of volunteers, including Brotherhood members if possible. There's some stuff I think they can help with."

Hazel looked up at him quickly then nodded. "Alright, I'll see what I can do."

"You do realise that if you're asking for volunteers, there's a good chance the spy will join your group? And they could ruin everything?" Cody said, looking sceptical.

Jesse shrugged. "If they do, then they do. We'll handle that when the time comes."

Cody looked steadily at Jesse for a moment, as if trying to work out if he was crazy. I didn't blame him.

"Fine," he said finally. "Well I'm guessing Blake and some of his crew will be going along."

"Definitely," Blake said with a huge grin on his face. I don't think I'd ever seen him so excited. "Me and my guys wouldn't miss it for the world."

"And I want to keep an eye on you, so I'm sending Percy."

Percy looked startled: "What, don't you want me here?"

Cody looked at him levelly. "I don't trust Jesse not to mess everything up. Make sure he doesn't, please?"

Percy frowned then jerked his head sharply. "Sure."

"Finally, if you do succeed there'll be a ton of organising to do, so take Kyle as well. With some of the Brotherhood, will that be enough?"

Jesse counted on his fingers, silently mouthing the numbers. "Should be," he said. "We'll leave tomorrow. Give us three days to get there, then start broadcasting as much information as you can about the Chickenator."

"Fine." Cody rolled his eyes. "This is going to be a disaster."

CHAPTER 21

JESSE: Operation Henhouse Hustle

It was much easier to sneak out of Aberdeen alone. The first time I escaped I'd crawled along the lines of abandoned cars that still clogged the A96. It had taken ages and by the end I'd been filthy and dying for a shower. But by the time the line of cars had ended I'd been out of Aberdeen, far away from any sentries.

That wouldn't work with such a large group. It would only take one person being careless and we'd be all be spotted. So I'd asked friends to make a diversion on the other side of town and we were able to sneak out unseen.

After that we tried to stay off the road, but close enough that we wouldn't get lost. We slogged through fields, tripped over tree roots and got our clothes snagged on wire fences. After an hour of this we were all moaning under our breath. Even Blake. I guess this adventure wasn't as exciting as he'd hoped.

Rayna walked next to me, quiet to begin with. I was just delighted to have my best friend by my side again.

"So what's the plan?" she muttered to me.

"I can't tell you," I muttered back. "I told you."

She gave me a look. "But I'm not the spy."

"No, but they might be lugging in. We need to make sure they don't get wind of it. It's going to be touch and go, especially once we're inside the barn. It's huge and we have to get upstairs to the control room before the chickens know we're there."

"How do you know where the control room is?"

Drat. I'd already given away more than I planned to. "I was captured. I escaped."

"What?" She turned and stared at me. "You got caught? Why didn't you tell me?"

"It didn't come up."

She glared at me, half frustrated, half curious.

"How did you get out?" she finally asked.

For a moment I was back in the chickens' control room. It was located in the barn's hayloft, with rows of computers tucked underneath a big screen. It had been filled with Commandos, keeping me under tight guard. I looked at the screen levelly. King Cluck stared back at me.

"Final answer?" he squawked. "You said you had information for me, that you wanted to be on the winning side. And now you won't open your beak."

"Yes." I tried to keep my face smooth, not revealing any indication of what I was thinking. I felt like spinning around, looking frantically for an exit but I couldn't show weakness. "Turns out I don't have anything else to say."

"This is just the first step you know. Once we control Turk— I mean Chicken, we'll finally be in a position to cross the water. Our wings will darken the sky and the Allies will fall at our beaks and claws. We'll peck out every one of them and then we will rule the roost in this world—"

King Cluck's cackle was cut short when an alarm began blaring through the barn.

A Commando scuttled up the stairs into the control room. "There's a riot in prisoner containment! They're trying to get loose!"

"Guards, stop them!" King Cluck screeched across the screen. "They must not be freed. They shall stay in the cages we put them in!"

Most of the Commandos dashed out of the room, leaving only a few guarding me. King Cluck turned his beady eye back to me. "As for you. If you want your brother to be safe, you'd better stick—"

"Shut up," I muttered and hit a button on the control desk. The screen went black and I spun around to look at the Commandos. They crept forward, inching closer before flapping towards me in a mad rush. One leapt for me but I dodged away and it went fluttering into the corner. Feinting to the right I jinked around the rest and ran for the stairs.

There were flashing lights everywhere and complete chaos as I half fell down the steps then fled across the hangar towards the door. The Commandos almost caught me but some escaped prisoners leapt on them, temporarily pinning them to the ground. I thought I recognised some faces but there was no time to thank them as I sprinted through the door.

"Jesse?" I blinked and was back in reality. Rayna was

looking at me, concerned. "Are you OK? I asked how you escaped."

"Yeah." I shook my head, snapping out of it. "Yeah, I'm fine. Um… right, escape. Some guys caused a diversion and I was able to get out. I couldn't take anyone with me though."

She was about to ask something else when one of the Brotherhood ran up. "Catcher," he panted, "in the road ahead."

"Come on," I said, grateful for the interruption. "We'd better go check it out."

It was an old one, a basic round body covered in dents and welt marks. It was standing by the road, not moving, facing down towards Aberdeen.

We stopped for a quick conference.

"This isn't good," I hissed. "We need to get past there. The only possible way over this hill is by the road."

"Can't we just walk through the woods or around it?" Rayna asked. There were groans from the rest of the group at the prospect of more cross-country hiking.

I shook my head. "That's the Tyrebagger. It's big and it's steep. The best way over it is by the road. We could try going around it but I don't know the way; we'd probably get lost and we have to get to the barn the day after tomorrow or we'll miss Cody's diversion."

"Can we take it out?" Blake asked, one hand on his shock-stick.

"Bad idea," Hazel said. "The chickens would notice that one of their sentries was missing. We might as well wave a huge flag saying we're on our way."

"Well, you come up with an idea," Blake said, all trace of his earlier friendliness gone.

Hazel looked at the ground, her face twisted like she'd bitten into a lemon. "There's only one thing to do. We have to let one of us get taken."

Instant silence. We all stared at her, shocked.

Rayna found her voice first. "What?" she asked.

Hazel shrugged. "It's the only thing to do. Once the Catcher gets one of us it'll wait around for a bit to see if there are any others then it'll have to take the prisoner back to the barn. That'll leave the way clear."

"And it won't find it suspicious that there's a kid out here—" Rayna began but Blake interrupted her.

"Not if it was one of the Brotherhood," he exclaimed. "They could just say they wanted to rejoin the flock or something. They'd buy that."

"How can you say that?" Rayna turned on him, furious. "How can you think giving up anyone is OK?"

"No, he's right. I'll do it." It came from one of the Brotherhood, a boy I vaguely recognised as Eric.

Hazel turned to him, solemn. "Are you sure?"

He took some gadgets out of his pack and handed them to Hazel. "What they're saying makes sense. One of us has to. I'll do it."

I walked over and patted him on the shoulder. "We'll get you out of there in a few days," I told Eric. "Stay strong."

Rayna looked aghast. "Are we really doing this? Is everyone OK with this?"

"Cody would agree," Percy pitched in gruffly.

And everyone seemed convinced. The Brotherhood all hugged Eric and patted him on the back, while Blake, Percy, Kyle and the others stood around nodding sagely. Then they parted and Eric walked forward.

We gathered in some trees to watch. Eric shuffled through a field and onto the road, around a bend so the Catcher couldn't see him. He brushed himself down a bit then walked up the road.

The Catcher watched him as he approached, not moving until Eric was right in front of it. Then it bent its head sharply down and stared at the boy. There was a moment's pause then its beak was open, moving forward. In a brief off-white blur, Eric was gone.

We stared silently at the Catcher for a while then it spread its wings and took off. It wheeled once in the sky then headed north, towards the barn.

"Come on," I jolted everyone back to reality. "We'd better get walking if we want to make it to the cave by nightfall."

"Jesse, wait." Hazel ran up to me. "A member of the Brotherhood's just been taken. Can't we take a moment?"

I looked at her and winked. "It's better not to brood on it," I said. Then I turned around and walked away.

We holed up inside a cave that night, with the ruins of my previous fire still waiting for us. There was an overpowering smell of blackberries, which grew on bushes all over the Tyrebagger. Before it got dark I'd taken a group out to gather some. Kyle boiled them up and made a sort of berry soup. It felt weird to eat but tasted delicious.

Rayna had gone off to get wood for the fire; out the corner of my eye I saw Blake follow her.

This was it. I nodded to Hazel and we both got up and followed him out.

"We can't trust them." The words floated through the trees once we got outside.

"Not this again. Look, Blake, I've told you plenty of times. We've got to. They're on our side. One of them sacrificed themselves for us today."

"Nope." There was a snapping sound as Hazel and I moved closer. "Don't you think that was a bit easy? I mean, who would get eaten by a Catcher voluntarily? Any normal person would fight against it. But that kid just went meekly. He wanted to do it. I think they're working with the chickens. We just can't trust the Brotherhood."

Hazel ran from my side and dashed into the trees ahead of me. I followed her and burst into a small clearing, where she was glaring at Blake and her sister.

"Is that really what you think? Despite everything we've done for you? You won't trust us, no matter what?"

"Wait, Hazel, I—" Rayna began but Blake overruled her.

"Yes," he said, staring at her, "I'll never trust you."

"Then you can do this on your own." Hazel turned and flounced into the trees. The three of us exchanged a shocked look and ran after her.

"Wait! Hazel!" Rayna grabbed her arm and swung her round. "You can't go. We need you."

"And yet you don't trust us. We've done everything we can for you and it's not enough." She wrenched her way free and strode back to the fire. "Well, I guess it's time we stopped trying. Come on guys," she said to the Brotherhood. "We're going home."

With that, she and the rest of the Brotherhood moved off into the woods. I followed the white of their robes until they vanished from sight and were truly gone.

I smiled. Everything was going according to plan.

CHAPTER 22

RAYNA: Operation Henhouse Hustle

My sister's always been a bit of a drama queen, but I still couldn't believe she'd stormed off like that, taking half our team with her. What was she thinking?

After the Brotherhood left, we all traipsed back inside to the campfire and sat down. We had some more berries but the previously sweet taste had turned sour in my mouth. The chatter of before had died. Even Jesse didn't try and tell any jokes, possibly a first for him. We all just sat around, picking at food, until it was time to go to bed. We posted sentries, two at a time, assigned randomly to stop any spies from reporting in, and got what sleep we could.

The morning was more of the same. It was supposedly just under 24 hours until our attack on the chickens' headquarters, but you wouldn't have thought it from all the subdued expressions. Jesse quietly gave us our instructions.

"OK, tomorrow, first thing in the morning, Cody is going to start broadcasting information about the

Chickenator to the Allied armies. It'll be technical spec, what tactics we used to take it down, everything that the chickens don't want them to know. We hope they'll react by sending everything they have to take out the signal, leaving their base vulnerable. We have to be there at the exact moment they leave to take advantage, but if we're too close for too long we could be found. So we're going to march to a farmhouse nearby, hide for most of today and set out in the middle of the night. Is that OK with everyone?"

They all nodded and we moved out.

We had to stick to the road, but Jesse was right. There were surprisingly few patrols this far out in the country. We had a nice, wide view of the surrounding countryside so if some chickens did appear we would be able to see them coming. It might not do us much good – the road was bordered by a steep slope on one side and a big drop on the other – but we would at least be forewarned.

We passed by a village called Blackburn, which had been completely trashed by the chickens. I wondered if Stonehaven, the town closest to where I used to live, had been treated the same way. I doubt my home was still standing; it used to be a chicken farm. After Blackburn we slogged towards the next village, a place called Kintore. We skirted around it, off the dual carriageway and over a few fields until we finally arrived at the farmhouse. By the time we got there I was looking forward to a rest. The door was open, and we all trooped in and crashed in the living room.

I hadn't had a chance to talk to Jesse since the night before, so while everyone else was sinking into chairs and claiming sofas I pulled him into the dining room and closed the door. He looked at me concerned. "Are you alright?" he asked, placing a hand on my arm.

I shook my head. "Of course I'm not alright. My sister is out there somewhere and I don't know if she's safe or not. And I drove her away."

"No you didn't," he said to me. "It was bound to happen sooner or later. It's my fault for not stopping it."

"I just don't know what happened. One moment Blake was being Blake, and then she was there and then... What do we do now? We've just lost half our group!"

"There's only one thing we can do," Jesse said reassuringly. "We've got to go on with the plan."

I laughed a bit. "The plan," I said. "The plan that you can't tell me about because there might be a spy in our group."

"Yeah, that plan." He gave me a crooked smile, which grew serious. "So who do you think it is?"

"Well, it's got to be either Blake or Percy, hasn't it?" I asked. "They're the only two left that are on the council. Unless it really was Hazel. Or Kyle?"

"Technically Percy isn't on the council."

"Yeah, but you know he does everything Cody asks

him to do, and he's always there in meetings at Cody's side. If Cody's the traitor then Percy might as well be. I mean, why else send him? He's too useful to Cody to risk him on a mission like this."

"I guess," Jesse mused. "Unless that wasn't the point."

I had risen to my feet and started pacing. At Jesse's words I turned towards him. "What do you mean?"

"Well, look at our group." Jesse spread his hands. "We've got Blake and his best chicken hunters. We've got Kyle, who's fantastic at organising, rationing and cooking. We had the Brotherhood, who knew everything there was to know about chickens. Maybe Cody didn't select this group just to try and free the people in the barn. Maybe he put us together so that if everything goes wrong, if the Catchers take Aberdeen, our group will still survive."

"So you're saying he didn't put Percy in our group to keep an eye on us, he did it so Percy would be safe?"

"Makes the most sense to me."

I thought it over. "Jesse—" I began, but before I could finish there was a scratching at the door. There must be someone on the other side.

Jesse put a finger to his lips. "There's one good thing that we know," he told me.

I knew what he was thinking. What if the spy was on the other side of the door, listening in to our conversation?

"What is it?" I asked.

He tiptoed over to the door, all the while still

talking. "Well, we didn't see any patrols today. None whatsoever. And you know what that means?"

"The spy can't have reported in yet."

"Yup." He took a tight hold of the door handle. "Otherwise they would have come for us. Now, if the spy was in Aberdeen there's a pretty good chance they would have reported in by now. Which means the spy might be someone in our group who just hasn't had a chance yet."

He pulled the door open in a sudden quick heave and someone tumbled in. Someone who must have been leaning against it, able to hear every word.

"Hello, Blake," Jesse said calmly. "Did you hear everything OK? Any questions?"

Blake scrambled to his feet, his face red. "I just wanted to know what's going on," he said. "I want to know the plan once we get to the chickens' headquarters. Is there any reason why I can't know that?"

"Yes, lots of reasons," Jesse replied. "For one, we wouldn't want you reporting back to the chickens. If you were the spy."

Blake's face turned a darker shade of red and he took a step towards Jesse. Fearing a repeat of last night I put a hand on his arm and held him back. Forcefully.

"Come on, Blake," I muttered. "You've been caught and you have to admit it looks suspicious. Just ignore Jesse and get over it."

I thought for a moment he wasn't going to listen to

my advice, but then he took a deep breath and exhaled. Turning to me, he nodded.

"You're right, Ambassador," he said respectfully. "I'm sorry."

Then he turned away and walked off to get some sleep, leaving me more than a little confused.

CHAPTER 23

We turned in early, and all got what sleep we could, which wasn't much. I spent most of the night wondering who the spy could be. It had to be someone among us. Could it really be Blake? He always seemed to be around when I needed him. I had come to trust him and I somehow couldn't see him betraying us.

When Jesse woke me up I was stiff and grumpy. "What?" I moaned at him, still mostly asleep.

"Come on, it's time to go," he said then handed me something brown and hot. I took a big gulp and found it was tea, milky and sweet. "Kyle made it."

I didn't really like tea. Mum had never let me have any at home, saying it stunted your growth, so I had never developed a taste for it. But as I drank deeply I could feel energy flowing back into my limbs. It woke me up. I didn't enjoy it, but at least it woke me up.

Everyone else was similarly roused and eventually we got on our way. Most of us were half asleep and tousle-headed. All except Percy, who looked geared up for action as usual, and Jesse, who was beginning to look nervous. I really hoped his plan worked, whatever it was. If it didn't then we'd probably all be gobbled up.

It was a good hour before we got near to the barn. Jesse took us through the woods, walking confidently ahead. I'm pretty sure we got lost at least once and passed the same pine tree about four times but eventually we got there.

Finally our target was in our sights. Jesse wasn't kidding. It was just an enormous barn. It felt kind of odd, seeing it over there, beyond the wide, golden fields of corn. Beside the barn was a small farmyard cluttered with equipment of various sorts, and the buildings sat in a large field. Surrounding the field was a high-wire fence. Take out the prison-style fence and it could be a farm scene from a toddler's picture book. It did not look like the place where huge metal monsters held our parents and friends captive.

"OK, here's the plan." Jesse gathered us all together at the edge of the wood where we were hiding. "We'll split into two teams. Percy will lead one and go round to the other side of the compound. The Ambassador, Blake and I will lead the other and attack from the front. Percy's team will cut through the fence then spread out and hide in the cornfield. My team will wait by the front gates. That way we'll hit the chickens in a pincer move. Once the diversion starts, most of the chickens should take off and head towards Aberdeen. There should only be a few left after that. I've got some of those egg grenades that the chickens gave the

Brotherhood. I'll use them to blow the doors off the barn so we can get everyone out – and there should be enough to take out any remaining Catchers and Commandos too. Percy, you've got your gloves."

There was a pause. "Well, aren't you going to give us some grenades?" Blake asked.

Jesse shook his head. "No. I can't trust you with them. I really don't want a traitor with a grenade. Any more questions?"

No one replied, but they didn't look happy. Percy took his team of five and disappeared round the back of the compound. Jesse took us even deeper into the woods and ordered our five to keep watch. I drew him aside.

"Jesse, this plan sucks," I told him.

He looked at me innocently. "What do you mean?"

"You know what I mean. We're *hoping* the spy hasn't already told the chickens what we're doing. We're *hoping* their defences will be weak enough for us to break in there. Even if there are three Catchers left that'll be enough to finish us. And what about all their Commandos? The plan is totally useless."

He sighed. "Look, I can't risk anything more complex. This is the best we can do."

"But this is insane! We can't hope to succeed like this!"

"This is the best we've got, Rayna. It might work. This could be our only chance to get our families back. Do you understand? I need this. Just trust me—"

He stopped abruptly. He'd got so impassioned, he was almost yelling. He lowered his voice. "Come on. We don't want to miss our opportunity."

The conversation was clearly over. We walked back over to join our team.

Almost an hour passed before anything started to happen. One long hour to think over what Jesse had said.

I had a terrible feeling about this. It wouldn't take much for everything to go wrong. Jesse had been right yesterday. Kyle, Percy, Blake and his hunters. We had a lot of good people with us. Enough to keep our group going. But we could just as easily be grabbed by the chickens. I was tempted to call off the mission—

Then all at once there was movement. Catchers came pouring out of the barn, running and flapping their wings. In minutes they were in the air. Their droning made the ground shake and the trees quake.

"I guess Cody's got his broadcast underway," Jesse shouted to me above the roar.

It took about a quarter of an hour for all the chickens to pass overhead. I was surprised to see so many of them. I hoped Cody's defences would stay strong.

Finally they stopped coming. Jesse waited for a moment then raised his head.

"Come on," he hissed. "Let's do it."

With one of our team left behind on lookout duty, the rest of us scuttled towards the gate. Once there, Blake pulled a set of wire cutters out of his bag and started chopping through the gate. After a tense few moments we were done and through. A road wound up through the cornfield but we couldn't follow it for fear of being seen. So we hunched down and stalked through the plants alongside it. Inch by inch we edged towards the barn.

"This is what I'm talking about," Blake hissed excitedly. "Finally showing the chickens who rules the roost."

And that's when everything started to go wrong.

A Catcher rounded the corner of the barn. We instantly flattened ourselves against the ground, waiting with bated breath until it moved on.

But then a figure appeared in the distance, yelling and waving. "They're over here! And over there! They're trying to free the grown-ups."

It was Percy. The traitor.

I shot upright and sprinted towards him, hoping somehow to reach him before the chicken noticed. My sprint ended in a lunge for Percy, but he sidestepped out of the way. My outstretched fingers brushed the leg of his trousers, but I landed on the ground with a hard thump and he slipped away, still running towards the Catcher, still yelling. Jesse leapt up and raced after him, hoping to get to him before the Catcher heard.

He was too late.

I saw, as if in awful slow motion, it turn its head and regard the two of them. It let out a loud squawk and more Catchers thudded out of the barn. Jesse saw them and turned around, trying frantically to back-pedal. I heard Blake shouting at his hunters to attack the Catchers. I ignored them.

"Jesse!" I screamed, reaching out a hand to him.

He turned to look at me, and another Catcher came screeching out of the sky. It landed hard, taking a few bouncing steps to reach his side. I recognised it as the same one that had taken Eric. Its head came up, it looked around briefly and then it struck.

Its beak plunged down, the sharp tips sinking into the dark earth and digging furrows as it closed with a snap. I tried running towards it but the Catcher's eyes flashed, and I stumbled to the side to avoid the laser blast. Then its head was rising, leaving behind the small hole we all recognised. Up and up its head went, further and further out of my reach. Then with a single fluid motion it swallowed with an abrupt gulp.

I stared at it, bewildered for a moment. All that was left were beak marks in the ground.

Jesse had been caught.

CHAPTER 24

My best friend was currently trapped in a metal chicken's gut and there was a very good chance I'd never see him again. In that moment I was back, seeing Hazel, Sam and so many others I'd known being taken. I wanted nothing more than to sink to my knees and surrender. Give up the fight.

But that wasn't how we would survive. The screams and cries of panic coming from the woods reminded me of the others in our group, the ones I could save. With some organisation and a lot of luck some of us might be able to escape.

I could give up later. To quote Jesse, *Right now there were some feathers to ruffle.*

As I turned back to the woods I saw Percy standing there, gloating. He ran into the trees. With a liquid burst of anger I sprinted after him.

I followed him into a nearby patch of trees. The branches whipped past my face and I almost thought I'd lost him, but when I charged into a clearing he was standing there, looking at me smugly.

"Well hello, Ambassador. Ready for the rematch?"

"Are you kidding?" I stopped in disbelief. "All this, just because I once beat you in the chair-wrestling match?"

He shook his head. "Oh no. This is just an added bonus."

"What were you thinking?" I snarled, stalking towards him. "What does Cody think he can gain from this?"

Percy's expression turned ugly. "Cody has nothing to do with this. I'm not his slave, no matter what the rest of you think. I'm his friend but I don't have to do every little thing he tells me to."

"So you betrayed him? Why?" I kept walking forward, getting closer and closer.

"I didn't betray him. I'll get out of this, the chickens promised me that. I'll return to Aberdeen a hero, the only one to survive. Finally people will know my name."

I couldn't believe my ears. "That's what this is all about? You just want people to think you're a big deal?"

"Yeah, maybe it is." He stepped towards me as well. My hand tightened on my shock-stick. Just a little closer.

Blake burst into the clearing. "You've got him?" he asked. "We need to move. The chickens are heading into the woods."

"Could you give us a moment?" I said, not looking at him, eyes fixed on Percy. "There's no way I'm letting this traitor get away."

"Fine." Controlled anger edged Blake's words. "We'll hold the Catchers off but we can't last long. There are too many of them."

"I won't need long," I said. Then in one quick movement I drew my shock-stick and lunged.

Percy must have seen it coming. He sneered and batted the stick away with one of his gauntlets. "Finally. The rematch."

"Bring it. I can take you any day."

He moved forward, throwing a punch, but I skipped backwards. This would be over soon. One of us just had to tap the other and they'd be out cold.

"So were the chickens expecting our attack?"

"Well, they don't seem to have left their headquarters unguarded, like you and Jesse stupidly assumed."

"So you stood behind Cody, behind your friend, at council meetings and then you went running to the chickens with everything, hoping for a pat on the back? All just to make sure *you* were OK, no one else."

My mind was ticking, putting everything together. "It all makes sense. Except one thing. How did you know Glen was going to be in Garthdee? I never even told you."

"I was in the hospital when you told Deborah. And then Cody told me you were going to Garthdee, but on a different day. It wasn't hard to connect the dots. I just looked out for you leaving." He lunged forward, fists jabbing but I stepped back and they just missed.

"And you sold everyone out. Just to save your own sorry hide."

"I'm safe and so is Cody. They promised."

"They sent the Chickenator to take him out. They're pretty lousy at keeping promises. And you must have told them where he was."

"He didn't get taken, did he?"

"Think he's going to thank you? We're so close to getting the adults back. That would have made us safe."

He spread his arms wide, gesturing around him. I stayed calm, waiting for my opening.

"You think I'm doing this just for myself? Nah, I'm doing what's right. The world is better without the adults. I like the way things are."

I blinked. "How could you believe that? The world is awful."

"For you maybe. I had nothing before all this. I couldn't figure anything out at school; I kept getting in fights. No one looked up to me, no one called me a hero. But here? Here I'm a new person. Here I'm great."

And there was the opening. "Here you *were* great. And now you're not. You're just a traitor, a coward and once again you've messed up everything. And now you're going to get beaten by a girl."

He gave a great roar of rage and charged towards me. I took three small steps to the side, ducked down and swept out. His fists just missed my head then my shock-stick whirled out and tapped him on the back of his legs. There was a spark, and then he crashed to the ground, like a toppled tree.

I stood there, staring down at him. I'd won. I'd beaten the spy.

But without Jesse there it all felt pointless.

Blake ran back into the clearing, followed by some of his hunters. "That's it, we can't stop them any longer," he gasped, out of breath. "We have to do something now."

I looked at him and nodded. "We run. There's no way we can succeed. We just need to pull back."

He nodded and we were about to turn away when we felt the ground shake. A Catcher came bounding through the woods, forcing us back towards the farm, some lagging behind and getting dragged by their friends. We burst out of the woods in time to see another Catcher coming for us. We quickly changed direction, only to find another ahead.

It was no use. We'd been corralled. Five Catchers surrounded us, blocking all possibility of escape. Four moved in, mouths clacking while one held back and observed. I recognised it as the one that had eaten Jesse and I fixed it with a hateful glare. Even as the others blocked my view I stepped to the side, determined to keep focusing my hatred on it until the very last moment.

So I was in the perfect position to see its eyes glow red as it shot another Catcher in the back.

There was a moment of confusion and the injured Catcher very slowly fell over with a clang like a giant bell. The rogue Catcher took the opportunity to shoot another one, its eyes scything through the Catcher's legs.

There was a sudden blaring of alarms from inside the barn and the doors swung wide open, Commandos pouring out. They surrounded the rogue Catcher, eyes glowing and lasers charging. I saw it setting its feet firm, ready to go down fighting. I grabbed Blake, pulling him away.

"Now, while they're distracted," I said. "We have to escape now."

Then abruptly the back of the Catcher opened up and a platform folded out, two huge lasers mounted on it. Hazel manned one, Jesse the other.

I could see the huge grin on Jesse's face as he triggered his laser, sending a bright red scar across the line of Commandos in front of him. Hazel did the same, and the enemy had to retreat before them. There might be more of them but we had more firepower.

"Blake!" Jesse yelled across to us. Blake blinked once then seemed to snap out of it.

"How can we help?" he yelled back, hurrying over.

"Go get the prisoners. We'll keep them off your back."

Blake looked towards the barn, a grin of his own answering Jesse's. "Yes, sir," he said, saluting and then running off towards the fight.

"Could you go with him, Rayna, and take the rest of our team?" Jesse asked. "There's a set of stairs just inside the door. At the top is the control room. There's a green lever. The buttons beside it target threats and their defence system should automatically target us.

Pull the lever down and it'll shoot everything targeted. Push it up and it'll shoot everything else."

There was no time to argue. I guess I just had to trust them. I frowned at them both. "Alright. But after all this is over we need to have a talk."

Jesse laughed, more a wild bark than anything. "Count on it."

Then he and Hazel dived back inside their Catcher, closing all openings as it leapt into the air, bounding towards the enemy, causing alarm and chaos. The perfect diversion.

I sprinted towards the still-open barn door alongside Blake and his chicken hunters. Once inside the cavernous building, I took a quick look around and saw a flight of stairs, just like Jesse had described. As I lunged towards them, a swarm of Commandos burst out from another opening, followed by yet another Catcher.

With a battle cry Blake ran to engage them. "Go on up, Rayna. We'll deal with these guys."

I nodded and ran up the stairs while war cries and metallic thumps rang out below.

At the top of the stairs I heaved the door open and cannoned into a room that looked like an old-fashioned hayloft, full of computers with a huge television on one wall. In front of the screen was a large bank of buttons and levers. I saw the one with the green lever, just like Jesse had described it. Striding across the room I reached out for it.

"Stop!"

I paused, looking up. A chicken had appeared on the screen, one I instantly recognised from the televisions in the communications room: small red comb hidden behind a weird, oversized hat. King Cluck, the boss chicken.

"You don't want to do that, Rayna." His voice issued from hidden speakers all over the room, disorientating me. I ignored it, more creeped out by the fact he knew my name.

"Yeah right," I said, grabbing the lever, preparing to push it up.

"If you touch that lever you'll never see your family again."

That wouldn't have been enough to stop me; who believes a chicken? But their pictures suddenly flashed up on the screen: Dad, a large man with a wild beard; Mum, just as muscular, long hair tied back in a utilitarian ponytail. I stared at them, my hand frozen to the lever. Then I shook myself out of my daze.

"I'll just go cut them out of whichever cage you've got them locked in downstairs."

Their picture flashed away, replaced by the cockerel, his evil beady eyes glaring at me. "But they're not downstairs. They're not anywhere close. They're in our high-security compound in Edinburgh. And the only way you'll see them again is if you do what I say."

"You're lying. Why are they special?"

"Oh, *they* aren't special, Rayna. *You* are. You see I knew you'd be coming in the next few days. And I knew it was *you* that I had to deal with. Fighters like Blake, planners like Cody: they are only so useful. But you, you have commitment. You're the one who keeps getting back up, who keeps fighting. The rest I can deal with. It was so nice of you to bring so many of the best defenders in Aberdeen here, where I can so easily capture them. Your band falls here, quickly followed by Aberdeen. But if *you* escape I know I'll be fighting another resistance somewhere. Your fighting spirit won't stop, won't quit. So that's why I have to destroy it here and now."

Something thumped into the side of the building, sending dust drifting in lazy spirals from the rafters. I could hear desperate shouts, the firing of lasers getting quieter. Things weren't going well outside.

"I won't just give up here. I can't," I answered.

"Oh, but you can. You don't even have to do anything. Just step back, sit in the corner. Five minutes and we'll have rounded up the traitors in that Catcher and anyone else stupid enough to be still hanging around. Then I'll personally see to it that you and your sister are taken straight to your parents. You'll be together again. You want that, right?"

I thought about it for a moment. "I do want to see my parents. More than anything." The chicken seemed to smile. I looked up at it, my eyes burning, hot and furious. "So that's why I'm going to go down there and bust up every barn you have until I find them. Starting with this one."

King Cluck jerked backwards in surprise and opened his beak. I didn't give him a chance to say anything else.

I flipped the lever.

A low moan filled the air, thrumming through us. I could feel the hairs standing up on the back of my neck and heard a clattering as hidden shutters slid open all over the barn. The pitch of the whine increased, vibrating my teeth until it vanished.

There was a moment of silence and then, with a mighty roar, every weapon fired at once. I heard the tinkle of lasers hitting metal and I looked out the window to see the remaining Catchers and army of Commandos falling like dominoes. Others looked around in confusion then took to the sky, flying away as fast as they could.

Then came a sudden deafening silence.

And soon from below and all around a low roar swelled, building until the enormous barn shook.

Cheers. The prisoners were cheering.

We'd won.

CHAPTER 25

JESSE: Henhouse Hustled!

Aberdeen was a glorious mess. Once we'd set the captives free, all the Catchers and Commandos had swarmed the city, hoping to take it before we could get back. Cody had already gathered practically all the kids left in Aberdeen into the tenement block before sending the signal. When the chickens arrived, they found a building bristling with lasers, each one manned enthusiastically. Bits of the fallen war machines were scattered everywhere.

Once news of our victory got round, the surviving chickens scattered: chicken by name, chicken by nature.

Aberdeen was free.

And on our first day of freedom, we'd mostly been clearing up. I'd grabbed a Catcher head and lugged it along to the Brotherhood's warehouse.

"So the adults all got into cars and drove us here," I told Clucky. "It wasn't easy getting them all working and we had to abandon them in impassable roads but it got us back faster than you'd think."

"Flying is still faster," Clucky told me, flashing his wings.

I swore he was smiling. "Piloting a Catcher is so much fun. I wish I'd been on Catcher duty from the start." Clucky had piloted our Catcher during Operation Henhouse Hustle and flown Hazel back to Aberdeen as soon as we'd taken down the barn.

"You were really good at it," I said. "What are the rest of the chickens doing?"

He tilted his head to the side, connecting to the chickens' control signal. "They're pretty confused at the moment. Most of the remaining Aberdeen army are fluttering around Scotland, with no idea what's going on. King Cluck is furious that we managed to give away details of the C-800 model to the Allies. They're back to square one on technical development."

"How long do you think it will take them to regroup?"

"A while." His eyes glowed when he looked at me. "Not forever, but a while."

"Jesse."

I turned and looked at the entrance to the warehouse. Rayna stood there, with Hazel beside her. I heaved a sigh of relief. "Hi guys," I called out.

"Why are you hiding in here?" Rayna walked towards me.

"I'm not hiding. I'm just filling Clucky in on everything that happened."

"You're definitely hiding," Clucky said beside me. "This is the third time you've told this story. I'm about to fall off my perch."

I glared at him. Traitor.

"Come on Jesse, out with it. There's a party going on right now. Why aren't you there?"

"I'm happy for you guys, really I am..." It turned out Rayna's parents were in the barn with the others. King Cluck had been bluffing about keeping them in a top-security prison, desperate to save his own crispy skin. I didn't think I'd ever witness Rayna crying, but let's just say their reunion was an emotional scene.

"I haven't found Ethan," I admitted with a heavy sigh. "I searched the crowds for him – and my parents – but they weren't there."

Rayna rolled her eyes. "So you just gave up? You stomped your way across half of Aberdeenshire to find your brother but a crowd defeats you? Honestly."

And then another figure appeared beside her and Hazel.

"Sorry I'm late," my brother said, a huge grin on his face. "I was checking out your defences. They're awesome. I couldn't have done better myself and I need to get my hands on one of those lasers. Come on, Mum and Dad are waiting for us."

It was him, hair a lot longer and shaggier than when I'd last seen him, but the same boots, same jacket. Same sense of energy and good humour. He was looking a bit thinner than before and maybe a bit battered but it was my same brother.

I looked up at him. "Oh no. It's worse than I feared."

Ethan stopped in his tracks, the grin fading. "What? Aren't you pleased to see me?"

"Well, yes, but..." I shrugged. "You've got taller."

He regarded me gravely. "I don't think I have. I think you've actually got shorter. Which is amazing really. Maybe I should get you that dolls' house to live in."

"Tall jerk."

"Short moron."

"Lanky idiot."

"Tiny occasional table."

"Oh that does it." I charged towards him, and then we were wrapped in a big bear hug.

"Pine tree," I muttered into his jacket.

"Toadstool," he replied into my hair.

I could almost feel Rayna rolling her eyes again. "Alright, now that's sorted, let's finally get some food."

"Good plan." Ethan snatched something off a nearby workbench and strode away, a Catcher head under one arm. Hazel rushed after him, grabbing it and returning it to its proper place. I laughed and Rayna laughed with me. After weeks of slogging through fields and keeping secrets it felt amazing.

"So how's the party?" I asked Rayna.

"Pretty good. Kyle is organising all the food we can spare into big vats so there's plenty to eat, and Jeremy is back to help him. Sally got her crew to pick some fruit and veg to add to the cause. Sam and his sister have been reunited and they're helping out too."

The grown-ups were amazed at how well we'd been running things without them. For today, they seemed happy to sit back and watch us rallying around them.

"Any word on Glen or Noah?" I asked hopefully.

"Glen's over there with his family, and Noah's got his dads with him. They're a riot."

"How's Cody? What did he do when he found out about Percy?"

Rayna hesitated. "He's... unusually quiet. His parents are keeping a close watch on him in any case. They seem really proud of him."

We were quiet ourselves for a moment.

"Come on," Rayna said at last. "Let's eat."

I walked out into the sunlight, blinking. For the first time in months Aberdeen wasn't eerily quiet. Now there was a low buzz hanging in the air. I could hear laughing, chattering, even singing. The adults were back and we were safe – for now.

But we'd better not count our chickens before they hatch...

Read on to find out how Jesse and Rayna's egg-splosive adventure began in

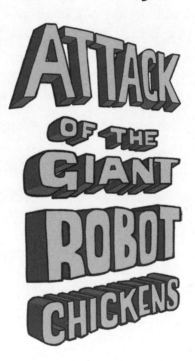

ATTACK OF THE GIANT ROBOT CHICKENS

CHAPTER 1

My big brother's hobby was the end of the world.

I don't know why, but he was fascinated by it. He'd talk about it all the time, all the different ways that civilisation as we knew it could come crumbling down. I had to listen to his plans to escape from tsunamis, meteors, floods, aliens and his favourite, zombies. He would never shut up about zombies. The walls of his room were covered with maps, and he'd drawn all sorts of lines and arrows on them. He was ready for anything.

I never got it. I mean, he was a normal sixteen year old the rest of the time. He hung out with his friends, he got good marks at school. He even had a girlfriend, though I think she was as confused about his hobby as I was. I mean, he wasn't even that geeky. Why would he have such a weird obsession?

I asked him about it once. He just shrugged.

"I like to be prepared," he'd said.

"For what?" I asked. "Zombies? Aliens? That's never going to happen."

He'd laughed at that. I can still see him, standing above me, the light shining off his glasses and his blond hair. "I guess you're right."

"So why do you do it?"

He'd sat down to tie up the laces on his boot, bringing himself down to my level. "I guess I just like the way it makes me feel. Safe. Like I'm prepared for anything, you know?"

I thought about that for a moment. "That's kind of weird," I told him.

He'd laughed again. He was always laughing. He never took anything really seriously. "Yeah. But everyone's a bit weird." He'd stood up again, kicking his feet a few times to make sure that his shoes stayed on. "Come on, little brother. Time to go to the movies."

Then he'd ruffled my hair and we'd left.

That had been eight months ago. I hadn't seen him since.

I shook myself out of my memories and looked around. Sam and Mike were standing above me, on the stairs that led to the upper floor of the Central Library. They were slouched against the wall, trying to show how unbothered they were by everything, but I could see how tense they were. So I decided to lighten the atmosphere with a joke.

"Hey guys, have you heard this one before?"

They both turned and looked at me, not impressed. I wasn't surprised. No one around here had a sense of humour.

"So there was this library, a bit like this one, only with a librarian. And one day a chicken walked in."

"Shut up, Jesse," Sam said. He was the leader on this expedition because he was the oldest. He was also a lot taller than me, though just about everyone was. That didn't mean I had to listen to what he had to say.

"So the chicken walks up to the counter and says to the librarian, 'Book, book.'"

Sam tried to ignore me and said to Mike, "Why do you think they haven't turned up yet?"

"Dunno," said Mike. I'm not sure why Sam bothered

asking. 'Dunno' was one of the only things that Mike ever said. Rumour was that it was his first word.

"So the librarian gave the chicken a book and it walked out the door. The next day it came back and the same thing happened. It walked up to the librarian and said, 'Book, book.' The librarian gave it another book and it walked out the door."

Sam continued to talk over me. "I mean, we've got the food they were asking for. They should be here."

I didn't give up. "This kept happening day after day and eventually the librarian begins to wonder where all his books are going. So the next day, as usual, the chicken comes in, goes up to the counter and says, 'Book, book.' The librarian gives it a book and it turns around and walks out of the door. But this time the librarian follows the chicken."

Sam gritted his teeth. "Seriously, Jesse. Shut up."

"He follows the bird and it goes out of the library and down the road. Then it goes down a farm track, still clutching the book under one wing. It reaches the farm and struts over to a pond. In the middle of the pond is a frog and scattered around it are all the books that the chicken has been taking out of the library. The chicken goes up to the frog and puts its present on a lily pad, going, 'Book, book.' And the frog takes one look at it, shakes his head and says, 'Reddit, reddit.'"

I beamed up at the other two. They failed to burst into laughter. They didn't even chuckle. They just glared at me. I swear the end of the world does something awful to people's sense of humour.

Lewis and Greg *might* have accidentally summoned Loki, the Norse god of mischief. Not to mention his hammer-wielding big brother Thor, trapped in the boys' garage... But it wasn't their fault!

With a gang of valkyries chasing them from St Andrews to Asgard, can the troublesome twosome outwit Loki and save the day?

 Also available as eBooks

discoverkelpies.co.uk

Mischievous fairies? Smelly troll? Werewolf snatching your sheep? Email the Really Weird Removals company!

Luca and Valentina's Uncle Alistair runs a pest control business. But he's not getting rid of rats. The Really Weird Removals Company catches supernatural creatures! When the children join Alistair's team they befriend a lonely ghost, rescue a stranded sea serpent, and trap a cat-eating troll.

Visit **reallyweirdremovals.com** for help with your paranormal pests.

 Also available as an eBook

discoverkelpies.co.uk

Fergus can't believe it when his brand-new watch starts going backwards. Then he crashes (literally!) into gadget-loving Murdo and a second mystery comes to light: cats are going missing all over the neighbourhood.

As the two boys start to investigate, they find help in some unexpected places.

 Also available as an eBook

discoverkelpies.co.uk